FRANCES TURK

A VISIT
TO MARCHMONT

Complete and Unabridged

ULVERSCROFT
Leicester

LARGE TYPE EDITION

First published 1964

First Large Print Edition
published September 1977
SBN 0 7089 0046 1

Published by
F. A. Thorpe (Publishing) Ltd.
Anstey, Leicestershire
Printed in England

Love is
a time of enchantment:
in it all days are fair and all fields
green. Youth is blest by it,
old age made benign: the eyes of love see
roses blooming in December,
and sunshine through rain. Verily
is the time of true-love
a time of enchantment — and
Oh! how eager is woman
to be bewitched!

PART ONE

THE DIG

1

DIARMID RIALL closed the top drawer of his desk and turned the key in the lock. He slipped the key into his pocket and looked round the large upstairs studio. For the first time for many years he was taking a holiday. Let the countesses and the producers and the society hostesses ring up. He would be in Ireland, having a royal time with Padraig.

Royal was the correct word. The old house in the midst of the green pastures, with the purple hills rising behind it, the rolling Atlantic billows not far distant, was royal indeed. Its name confirmed its status: Marchmont Royal.

He prowled round the studio, glancing at the various décors and designs on the easels. There was the vast Egyptian scene he had created for Lady Hannington, there the Venetian palace for Lewis Hope at the Greuzer Galleries; that had caused a sensation; Jordan Joyce's panegyric in the *New Theatre* had prompted a craze; everybody must have their rooms transformed by Diarmid Riall.

He slaved like a navvy. All the hours of every day and often half the night, until Lewis foretold a collapse, but Diarmid had been insatiable; he had been on the crest of a wave, the man of the moment; the ultimate achievement had been the Palladian adornments at the Castlehams in June.

Lewis was right. They had been undergraduates together at St. Withburga's in Cambridge, occupying adjoining rooms in Inner Court. While Diarmid had been undecided on his profession, Lewis was daily in the Fitzwilliam and other galleries, already on the way to his position as art dealer and acknowledged successor to Adam Greuzer of Milsom Street. An undergraduate rag had been the means of confirming what had been floating in his mind but till then had not crystallised; his décor, thought up in the small hours on rough sheets of drawing paper, had been an outstanding success and drawn long columns in the local press; but the beginning had been less fortuitous. Masters like Cordot and Wessell had been wary of a youngster, and Irish withal, though he had not been in Ireland for eleven years; they wanted no amateur stealing their thunder with his unorthodox ideas. As in everything, it needed courage and perseverance and intense faith to "arrive".

Lewis had been unwaveringly good, and Jordan Joyce in his way, putting him in line for minor commissions. Here, for instance, was the design for the Freedom Ball which Leah Hope, Lewis' aunt, had run for her refugees and for which she had asked him to decorate the Aureolean Hall. He had taken Europe as his theme, and the result had been — one line in one newspaper. He chuckled, looking back on his thimble successes. The sun was shining through the large windows, suffusing the vast space with warmth. He expanded with the glow. Even before he began his journey, he felt a freshness in his veins.

The studio was a story in itself: he had

found the warehouse, dilapidated and dirty, cluttered with mortar and fallen tiles, and converted it from a workshop on the ground floor and this perfect working-room above. Small wonder men said he could do with a holiday. Oscar Meredith wanted to stage a space play at the *Venus*; would he do the décor? He rang Lewis. "I'm off to the moon. You haven't any space suits handy, have you?" When he got to Ireland, he must let the ideas simmer; here, in this mass of humanity, these choking fumes, he could not clear his mind sufficiently to allow the regions of space to intrude.

Providentially, Padraig's letter had come, a week before, dropping through his letter-box. He hardly knew Padraig, though they were brothers, for Padraig had spent his youth with the Riall side of the family and he had been sent to England to Aunt Ma-Ma and Uncle Victor, to the high narrow house in Victoria Road, St. John's Wood. That had been when their mother had been drowned in Clunare Bay and their father had turned from his sons and imprisoned himself at the Royal.

Ma-Ma — her real name was Maisie —

4

had not had children of her own and she took Diarmid with a strength and a purpose that might have overwhelmed a less resilient child. "For heavens' sake, Ma-Ma," Uncle Victor cried, "let him be. You can't alter nature," with that acceptance of fact that came to him in the bookmaker's office where he had seen the rise and fall of men with a rapidity Maisie could never have dreamt of. Diarmid was fascinated by him and added further to her dismay by sitting on the rug at his feet and storing his titbits in his capacious mind.

Victor Naismith did not reprimand him when he covered page after page of his penny exercise books with designs for refurnishing the rooms. After the sprawling, semi-ruinous expanse of Marchmont Royal, the house in Victoria Road was a kind of doll's house, choked with pot-pourri and Victoriana, and Diarmid's favourite game was to strip the rooms of their contents and refurnish them with suites and furniture he saw in the shops on his way to school. Later, as he grew up and either Aunt Ma-Ma or Uncle Victor took him to the West End or into Petticoat Lane he glimpsed the wider range available to adults, his tastes varied, but in those earliest days he sought refuge in his fancies and oddly enough found an ally in Victor. The advent of a boy into his household was as much a challenge to Victor as it was to himself. Both rejected, in measure, Aunt Ma-Ma's restrictions; both were, in her house, subjects of her suzerainty. Men to men, thought Diarmid now, remembering Victor with gratitude, his final fling with a toleration that neither condoned nor despised, but allowed in the nature of men a tossing wide of the curtains of respectability and admitting the sun of reaction.

The difference was that while it might have been expected of a Ruaidhri Riall, it was not expected of a Victor Naismith. Before that, however, there had been six happy years to enjoy, as unexacting as a passage through untroubled seas, as uneventful as the waves of Clunare Bay had been cruel and annihilating. It was Victor, not Maisie, who told him of the tragedy, when she had gone to a bridge evening, and they sat on either side of the hearth in the sitting-room. As a result, he was vouchsafed a somewhat hazy picture of Elinore Riall, asking endless questions until the clerk said: "She was a right, fine lady, Diarmid. You should be proud of her." Thereafter, he carried the picture in his mind, a right, fine lady of whom he had no shame.

He often wished, though, he had a portrait or a photograph, to stand on his work table, who would approve his efforts and congratulate him. When he reached Marchmont, he would find one and ask Padraig for the gift of it.

Padraig was a little clearer. He had come to England and called on Aunt Ma-Ma and Uncle Victor while a student at St. Kinan's, and had impressed his younger brother with his ability to discourse. The visit had lasted two hours; then he had gone, having laid a bet with Uncle Victor that, the latter winning, had begun the course of gambling which had culminated in his disappearance. That was something else to tell Padraig.

It was a good thing he was going to Marchmont. A spell in the west would revitalise him and reunite him to his father's land. He whistled suddenly and moved to the doorway as the telephone shrilled on his desk.

"No," he said swiftly, "I am going to Ireland, to Marchmont Royal, to my home where my blood runs free." Stupid, fanciful, Irish baloney! In the relief of the vacation, he was more Irish. "I am not here. I am away to Padraig." He opened the door and the telephone shrilled again. "I will not," he repeated, but it might be Lewis, wishing him a comfortable journey. He took up the receiver.

"Diarmid?"

"Hector, you hound! I'm just off to Marchmont."

"I hoped I would catch you before you left."

"I'm taking a holiday. I haven't had one for years."

The voice at the other end of the line was soothing, like the touch of a balmy breeze. "Give him my regards."

"I didn't know you knew Padraig."

"You would be surprised who I know."

"All right. I'll carry your regards across the sea and tell my brother how honoured

8

he is. Meanwhile, to what great moment do I owe this particular call?"

"I will tell you when you come."

"I am going to Ireland, Hector, in a couple of hours."

"I can tell you what I want to say in a quarter of that time. Not over the telephone, though. I never conduct business over the telephone."

"Begorra," said Diarmid, "is it telling you again I am setting out — ?"

"I have something for you to take with you."

"I know you of old. You'll inveigle me and I shall miss the boat and Padraig will be storming on the quayside — he's like my father; he blows up like a storm in the bay and the air hisses with his ire — and he'll never ask me again. I shall be an exile for ever . . . I haven't the time but I suppose I shall come. Another second and you'd have missed me."

"Another second did not pass," imperturbably.

He ran down the stairs. To Chester, his foreman, he said: "I'm off now. Mr. Burne has just rung. I'm calling on him on the way to the station. I'll be back in a couple

of weeks. You know my address? Marchmont Royal, Co. W— "

"Have a good time, sir," said Chester.

"I'm looking forward to it, indeed,"
and went out into the narrow lane in which
the warehouse stood.

Hailing a taxi in Simpson Street:
"Waddesdon Square, please, and hurry.
I have an hour to keep an appointment and
catch a train from Euston and I have to
go to Charles Street first."

The cabby grinned. "Leave it to me,
sir."

They were soon there. "I'll be out in
half an hour," said Diarmid, running up
the steps to the Georgian doorway and
ringing the bell. The square looked
secluded; already he had an idea for a
décor. All he wanted was a play . . . and
Hector Burne wrote plays under the
pseudonym of Conal O'Bridie.

"Come in, dear fellow."

Burne was an invalid. He lay on a
couch by the window, his work table
beside him, and a rug over his legs. His
hands and limbs were frail; there were
days when it seemed that a puff of wind
would blow him away but inside that

ailing frame throbbed a dynamic will that carried him into the realms of creation. His plays regularly delighted London; they were tight, well-constructed, well-characterised pieces contrived to make their audience sit up and not loll. Producers vied with each other to sign up the new Conal O'Bridie and the author remained quietly and industriously in his Waddesdon Square house, summoning friend and associate by telephone, guarded by his faithful Pratt who had been with him for years.

Diarmid crossed the room to the high window where the sunshine poured in and alighted on the thin ascetic face.

"I've twenty-five minutes," he announced.

"I see your taxi is prowling," replied Burne.

"He is my guarantee. Nothing matters when you have a new play. Is that it? You want me to do the décor?"

"Jeremy does."

"Egod!" Diarmid's lips creased into a smile. "A battle of the giants and Crooke is the winner. He's not swindling you, Hector?"

"I hope not," said Burne.

"Check up. Check and check again. That man comes from Stepney."

"While you come from Ireland! Between you, I shall need my wits about me. What's your price? Half a million?"

Diarmid chuckled. "Dare I?"

The other's eyes sparkled. "Diarmid Riall dare all and get away with it. You're going away? To set them all by the ears? To have the countesses and the dowagers panting on your doorstep? Clever man."

"I'm going because Padraig has invited me. I need a rest. What's the play? A square in London?"

"Too coincidental. Though I might."

"Is that it?" indicating a manuscript on the table. He leaned forward and took it. The title page fell open. "*The Irish Room.* So that's why. Did you say it was not coincidental?"

Burne's thin face warmed. "Touché. Who else could do it? Prosper? Wessell? They'd do the usual stuff, what the public thinks is Ireland. You'll do it authentically, with that touch of the master, that extra finish that is your hall-mark."

Diarmid saw the faith and hope in the other's stare. "It seems providential. Will Marchmont be the kind of place you have in mind?"

"I've never seen Marchmont. The play is in Dublin, not Co. W— ; it's a sophisticated play; none of your wild coasts and Irish leprechauns and illegal poteen. I had the idea after reading the Garrow case though it has no bearing on those events or any likeness to that affair."

"Mistaken identities?"

"No, relationships only. The clash of wills and personalities in a single house within a certain period of time; not like any of my other plays."

"I begin to see," said Diarmid. He felt the challenge rising inside him. A new venture, with Conal O'Bridie at the conception and he at the fulfilment. A pairing to set the critics talking! His eyes gleamed. His voice carried the timbre and pitch that it took in his most excited moments. "I appreciate your invitation, Hector."

"I've had a devil of a time with Jeremy. He wanted Prosper who would have ruined it. I have a proper regard for Sebastian Prosper — he triumphed in *The April*

Sun and in *Felicitations* — but *The Irish Room* is not his métier."

"I always think Crooke is similar to Aunt Ma-Ma, sugar sweet if the audience is respectful of his point of view but acid vinegar if there's a voice raised against him. I don't promise to read it for a week."

"I'll give you three weeks."

"Anything else I should know?"

"I don't think so. Read it and let me know." Burne indicated the cabinet in the corner. "What is this holiday? A mere whim, or pilgrimage, or a search for a theme? Pour me a Scotch. I don't normally at this time of day but if I'm not to see you for some weeks it's an excuse. I must ensure your participation. What was that you said as you came in? Plane trees. A square. It's creating a thought. What an extraordinary fellow you are. The ink is hardly dry on one script when you set a spark to another. Have you the sets in detail?"

"Hardly, but for what they're worth . . ." He took a pencil from his pocket and a pad of paper from Burne's work table and sketched rapidly. "If you can decipher them," proffering them. "The title you can choose. the plots and passes, but there's the motive."

"We'll go shares," smiling.

"If Jeremy agrees. Or Hassey, or Coke. We'll play them against each other. You're a wizard, Hector! I'm going to Ireland with my brain on fire. I thought I'd run dry."

"Nonsense," swiftly. "There's something taking you there."

"Padraig and some rambling affair about a 'dig'. He's got a party under Alec Codrill digging up Quilty's Pasture in the hopes of finding an old monastery. I thought when his letter came I might find some 'copy'. He sounded in need of brotherly support. Knowing the archaeologists, I fear he may be no longer master of his own house."

2

THE writing on the envelope had made him raise his brows. How long since Padraig had written? When Aunt Ma-Ma died.

"You may like to know Aunt Ma-Ma died last evening," he himself had written. "She was rambling in her mind and had not been her true self since Uncle Victor pawned the property and vanished like blue smoke. It was happier for her to go, though I was sad. The house seems empty without them."

The reply was short and sparse. "My regrets at the news of Aunt Maisie's death. I only saw her the twice, when I came over to England, and I must admit I was not attracted by her. She was nothing like our dear mother whose portraits I have. Nevertheless, you must feel your loss. In her odd way, she endeavoured to give you what she felt it her duty to provide." Diarmid felt that Padraig had written the truth but he felt also he might have infused more warmth and sympathy into the words.

This latest epistle, however, had nothing of condolence to send. Nobody had died, save a dog or two at Marchmont and possibly some pigs — Diarmid found difficulty in following the affairs of the denizens of his old home, the more so because his brother's handwriting was atrocious and well nigh unreadable — and what had happened appeared to be an invasion of a scale to be compared with the battles of old when the Royal was under fire from rival tribes or, diving into the dim relics of history, the Danes came marauding along the coast, attacking the local inhabitants and destroying the homesteads.

"We are overrun with creatures in denims and wool sweaters who wield venomous spades and measure with tapes and rulers and study the pastures and the ancient maps with a zest I find incredible to behold. The professor seems a cultured man, though particularly obtuse on any subject except archaeology, going about with a besotted expression on his features, bent over humps and hillocks that so far as I know have no significance at all. He has turned the library into a shambles and subjected me to a cross-examination of facts and figures and guesses and surmise that leaves me chasing my own wits. They are, they say, these crazy madmen, seeking the remains of St. Cuimin's abbey, but St. Cuimin, you may remember, held out on the Island of Clunare within two hundred yards of the spot where our mother was drowned with Cousin Colum. Though, can they see it? Begorra, Diarmid, if you have a week to spare, come and relieve me from their attention. Some sane thought in this whirling madhouse would be as welcome as Irish whisky."

Certainly, he was no longer master in his own house and Diarmid gained a whimsical amusement as the train carried him westward to Holyhead. In his brief-case was the manuscript Hector Burne had loaned him, three acts, carefully typed, with incisive instructions, maybe too clear for Jeremy Crooke who had his personal interpretation of directions. The partnership of the two constantly amazed him but the final presentations were proof of the love of the theatre which activated both men.

Hector was a cunning bird! Getting him there when he was off to the Royal and giving him no time to react. What kind of a room did Hector envisage? He folded away Padraig's letter and zipped open the brief-case. There must be hundreds of rooms in Ireland, yet none might fit the precise situation. Did Hector imagine there was one at the Royal? Or one in the village of Cloncobh? Or could it be merely the authenticity he required?

The characters were on the typewritten sheet. Lady Luke, an English countess. "Tall, fluttery, henna-haired, always with chiffon round her shoulders, silly, talkative, adolescent in bearing." Lancelot Luke, her son. "Overbred, inane, weak-chinned, pansy." Hector, my lad, was this the masterpiece one had expected? Father Flaherty, an Irish priest, once a convict. What had he to do with fluttering butter-flies? "Big, strong, rough, with the phys-ique of a horse and the mentality of a gnat." His room, maybe, in some back street, half-slum, the sole ornament a crucifix. Conspiracy? Smuggling? "Superintendent Boyle, a member of the police, with previous contact with Father Flaherty, broad, equable, with invalid daughter and wife dying of tuberculosis." The train rushed on towards Holyhead; Diarmid's leaping imagination kept pace with the wheels. A room at the police station. Another in the hotel in Connel Street; mother and son agitatedly pacing the pile carpet, every now and then going to the window. One in a Georgian house in Stephen's Green, outwardly serene, monument to an era . . . into it the clash of internecine warfare, natures driven almost mad by anxiety, fear, horror, crime. "Tim, an urchin from the docks, ragged, unprincipled, serving Father Flaherty as an acolyte." Serving also other people as a go-between, his underfed body slicing through back alleys, on to ships, down hatchways. Running errands for Superintendent Boyle, begging coppers from Lancelot Luke, the link between the grown-ups. An orphanage, the carpetless floor, the watchful, slinking eyes. A whole series of Irish rooms . . .

He was at Holyhead. He pushed the manuscript into his case and stood up to collect his luggage. "Porter," giving his instructions about his passage. The air was blowing in from the sea; the tang of the west invigorated. His heart and his nerves gave an involuntary leap. How often he had thought of returning to Marchmont and here he was at last on the harbour at Holyhead.

Four hours later, he was by the rail, taking in the scene at Dun Laoghaire. Soon, he was standing on the quay and feeling the uneven stones beneath his feet. There was no sign of Padraig, though he had half-expected there might be, but doubtless his brother had not liked to leave his house in the possession of the invaders.

There were other passengers in his carriage when he left Dublin and within moments he was engaged in conversation with them.

"You be Riall, you say?" one of his companions asked, a farmer from Dundoran. "From the Royal, beyond Cloncobh?"

"Do you know it?"

"I know of it."

"My brother lives there, Padraig Riall. Our father died several years ago and our mother was drowned in Clunare Bay when we were young."

"Och, I remember now. You be Diarmid, then?"

"Padraig writes me there's a dig on. He's bedevilled with shades of St. Cuimin."

"The saint of Clunare."

"The same," agreed Diarmid. "He's fulminating against these usurpers who insist that Cuimin had an abbey at Marchmont. Padraig's a scholar and he does not relish contradiction."

"Och, aye," said his companion. "Ruaidhri was a whale of a man."

"Padraig's like him in some ways. I can imagine extraordinary things happening in this mystical land."

"Padraig's a stickler now. I mind him in Dundoran of a St. Patrick's Eve. You be staying long?"

"A week or two. Then I must return. I'm an interior decorator and about to design a set for Conal O'Bridie's new play."

"Kathy and I always go to Dublin when there's a Conal O'Bridie at the Abbey. You're acquainted with Conal O'Bridie? I'd much like to meet that man."

"Come to see me next time you're in London and I'll take you round. Hector — that's Conal; O'Bridie's his professional name — would be pleased to see you. Most of the time he's chained to his couch so any intrusion from the outside world cheers him enormously. This is my address — or here's my studio; you might be interested to see it; it was a broken-down warehouse before I renovated it."

"I appreciate your kindness. The name's O'Grady. My brother's a solicitor in Cork and I have a nephew in London, training to be a dentist You'll be having callers, betimes."

"The more the better," smiled Diarmid. "When the professor gets obtuse, I'll be borrowing the car and coming over."

A further hour brought him to the outskirts of Dunphilly. There was only a country woman left with him who had been lulled by the rocking of the train into a heavy slumber. Should he wake her? He decided not; she deserved her rest. Gathering his bags, he stood at the door as the train slowed down.

On the platform was a thin-limbed, dark-haired, slightly stooping man talking to the station-master. Padraig held out his hand and introduced Mr. McEwan.

"It's pleased I am to see you, Mr. Diarmid."

"I'm glad to be here at last." He smiled

in his pleasure. "I'll be taking hold of that," gripping his brief-case. "It has Conal O'Bridie's new play."

"Indeed." Padraig was mildly interested. Mr. McEwan opened his eyes wide and obviously was eager to ask questions.

"Is Mr. O'Bridie well?"

"Full of beans," said Diarmid. He was trying to equate this station at Dunphilly with childhood memories and finding the past too distant. "I left him in labour with a fresh idea. The man's a marvel; he works like forked lightning."

"If I may say so, Mr. Diarmid, you haven't let the grass grow yourself."

"Don't tell me you've heard of that Venetian palace down here!"

"Indeed we did. The *Chronicle* ran an article."

"Padraig," he turned, rueful, "I thought I was coming for a rest."

"You'll have little rest with these con-founded diggers. Eh, McEwan? They're everywhere."

The porter carried the bags to the car and after being waved away by Mr. McEwan with a respectful touch of his hat Diarmid was transported along the narrow,

winding, high-banked roads to Marchmont Royal. The car was elderly, a legacy
from Ruaidhri but in good running order
and Padraig drove it competently. Over the
countryside hung a delightful languor that
Diarmid found relaxing.

"How have you been getting on? It's
years since you came to Victoria Road and
I saw you for ten minutes. Begod, we're
greater strangers than two men who live in
the same street. I don't feel I know you at
all."

"I find life at the Royal stultifying."

"I'm told you're like our father. A
farmer in the train from Dundoran told me
a mite about the Rialls of the Royal. Are
there journals in the library about this
ancient family? Leatherbound diaries by
our marauding forebears? I'm quite innocent," he said. "Being brought up by
Maisie Naismith did not prepare me for
ghouls. Uncle Victor's line was horses, the
running of. He was kinder, actually, than
Aunt Ma-Ma, not a bad chap at all. I
think I'd have gone off the rails if I'd been
tied to her for life."

"She was our mother's sister."

"Sure, I never knew how she could be,

though I knew little about our mother. Was there a mystery about her, with Cousin Colum? Aunt Ma-Ma hedged her so about with white angels I could never believe she was real."

"If anything, my upbringing was sterner and staider than yours."

"You saw Father, though. I never did, between our sending away and his death."

"When he wanted Uncle Patrick's advice; then I was shy of him and gained nothing from the visit. I came to the Royal a stranger, as you're coming now, and found it a morgue."

The western sun was sinking over the peaks of the hills and Diarmid's eyes were watching the shimmering haze. Streaks of red and gold overtopped the soft blues and spread a carpet of amber and russet over the intervening land. Somewhere ahead, at the foot of the Reek, stood the Royal, built of the same hard rock and stone.

"Every room but three was shut up," Padraig went on. "He had lived solely in the library and in a smaller one where he ate and in a slip of a dressing-room where he had a camp bed. There were no servants

26

as such. A woman and a girl came up from Cloncobh village."

"A kind of Miss Havisham?" The reading of *Great Expectations* had left a deep impression on Diarmid's mind. Victor had given him the book at Christmastide and he had read it gulpingly, sucking up the adventures of Pip with eager, devouring mind until he reached the point where Miss Havisham lived amidst her cobwebs and her dwindled glory.

"Hardly," smiled Padraig. He turned the car into a rough, overgrown drive.

"Where are the gates?"

"Long since gone. Tempest and storm demolished them before I came."

"I liked them," said Diarmid.

"I thought you did not remember."

"I remember them. Can't you replace them?"

"Hardly a necessity," remarked Padraig.

"Necessities don't matter. Why not, as a thank-offering when the diggers go? Where are they, by the way?"

"In Quilty's Pasture."

"I remember that. A bleak, flat, open, windswept plain bounded by the walls of Clonreagh."

"Our father built more walls. He planned to drain and cultivate the furthest half."

"I can't believe a monastery stood there."

"Codrill says so."

"Is he well-known?"

"He's a pest," said Padraig promptly.

"You can't see the dig from the house?"

"From the western rooms. Would you like that side?"

"Only if it catches the sun. I want the sun and the sea and the whole vast sky. One's view in London is restricted to roofs and chimney pots and while they're useful betimes — Cherry Anderley wanted roofs for her masque but it's unusual except in ballet and mime — I want other things at the Royal. Can I choose my room when I've seen the house?"

Padraig looked amused. "Don't rate the old place too high," he warned. "It's shabby and ill-kept and not as our mother had it. Very little 'royal' about it. Like the coat-of-arms in Dublin. Tawdry and despised."

The hint of disillusion was clear. Somewhere between the boyhood and today the past had misdirected. Padraig should emerge from his shell and find a purpose for his life. The few hours he had spent at Victoria Road had revealed a cleverness; why was he wasting his talents at Marchmont instead of writing a fresh page of the history of the Rialls?

"Why not find a wife? This place needs a host of children. If Father had kept us here instead of bundling us off like kittens to the well he would have been wiser."

"Have you done so badly? Would you be Diarmid Riall, interior decorator, if you had stayed at the Royal?"

"I daresay. While you'd have been a surgeon or a solicitor or dentist or some fine architect instead . . ."

"Instead?"

"That's presuming . . . You may be a great man for all I know. It's time we got together."

"You might have gone to Dublin and London but you wouldn't have gone to St. Withburga's. You wouldn't have met Lewis Hope or the other people you know. You would have drifted back here, as I did, after the war, to fall into its slough."

"It's very lovely," said Diarmid. "It's as well I've brought Hector's new play or I might have failed to return."

29

"I agree," replied Padraig.

The house was ahead in a slight hollow, surrounded by its trees, its circle of mauve hills and its overgrown gardens, sprawling, no particular period, impinging on his memory and claiming his love and his allegiance. The light-hearted banter that came naturally to his lips died in silence; the gap was infested with a wealth of feeling that threatened to choke him. Tears sprang to his lids, not tears of sentiment or longing, but of gratitude that he had come, that Padraig had sent for him, however belatedly, so that he was back before the days of Aunt Ma-Ma.

"Is the veneer so thin — ?" Padraig at his elbow.

"It's too lovely. Why did you never ask me before? Why have you kept it selfishly as our father did? By the saints, they were right when they said you favoured Ruaidhri, that in you he lived again. Aunt Ma-Ma had sense when she cursed the man who had enslaved her sister. I can hear her now. 'That man. Don't let me hear you mention his name'."

"You're a Riall," Padraig said. He had gradually slowed the car. "You're one of the family whatever else you've become. We're not so very different, you weaving dreams over the sea and commanding huge sums for enacting them, me weaving dreams here and living indigently. I cried when I came home, cried for what I had missed, what the Royal had become, what I should do now I was here, what I have since failed to do. Cried too, with impotence and rage, when it has proved too strong for me, too cruel and too harsh, too wild and too cursed, so that I've cringed as I cringed as a boy when the waves lashed the coast, when our father stormed like Lear through the rooms, cowered in fright and frustration . . . You have come, Diarmid, and I must welcome you and show you that Marchmont does not forget its manners." Slowly and haltingly, the fierceness had faded; the host took his place. "Marchmont has much to display, despite its occupancy by frenzied professors and long-haired youngsters. Do they all walk about like that, Diarmid? I appear to be an anachronism. I change for dinner whereas they — "

"Invaded by beatniks?" Diarmid relaxed. "It can take it. These stone walls can take anything. Didn't Professor Codrill ever imagine this was the abbey? It might well have been."

"The abbey," stated Padraig, "stood in Quilty's Pasture on a line due west of Kilmeenan Reek and due east of Murragh Pins. It was three hundred feet long and encompassed an area of twelve hundred square feet."

"Good Lord!" Following him up the worn stone steps, Diarmid exclaimed. "You must tell me about it. I sniff a germ of a drama for Hector."

"You'll have ample evidence of such while you're here," said Padraig.

He was introduced to Mrs. Sullivan who was Padraig's housekeeper and who had prepared his old room for him.

"Mr. Riall told me — "

Diarmid turned towards Padraig but the latter had gone into the library to see to the post which had arrived while he had been to Dunphilly. "I was going to choose my own room. It's many years since I was here." He was aware of alienable facets in Padraig. Almost, at moments, he would approach him; then in the flash of an eyelid he was a stranger behind another façade. Hector

Burne's soft utterances impinged. "A study in relationships." Good heavens! He was in a whirlpool of them already, and he had not met the madmen of the dig.

"Does the Professor sleep in the house?" he asked the housekeeper.

"He does. He and his staff have the west wing."

With all the wild scenery of the coast! The side he had wanted, with the view of Clunare where, long ago, a boating accident had deprived him of his mother. His quick, changeable anger rose up. Had he come all this way to be deprived of a room on the west side, to have his holiday marred by invaders from the east? Why must they upheave the soil and fill the silences with their raucous shouts? Padraig had got him here on false pretences. He could have concentrated on Hector's play. Lady Luke, Lancelot Luke, Father Flaherty, Superintendent Boyle, Tim. Put them all here, in this dark stone hall, and see what they did. His "nigger" of a moment ago was dented, as the picture played about in his mind. Was this the Irish room? Or the morning-room, facing the eastern sun, its mullioned panes flooded with a glow of exaggerated light? He turned to Mrs. Sullivan. "I'll have the eastern end, away from the pack."

"Your room was in the east wing, sir."

Lord, so it had been.

He bathed and dressed quickly, so as not to miss a moment more of Padraig's company than he might. It was unnatural they should know so little of each other. They could talk until the small hours and he would learn of Padraig's life with Uncle Patrick and in the Army and since the war ended. His dark brown eyes full of a sparkle, he ran down the stone stairway and into the banner-hung hall. Portraits and armour — his gaze capered merrily in what Lewis would call his Irish mood; everything was here, unchanged for centuries, cluttered with dust; Miss Havisham *in excelsis*. Pure history, fantastic bravery, dark deeds, false treachery. A setting for Christie or Simenon? Or a macabre drama, with stealth and queer minds its main ingredients?

"Good-evening," said a low cultured voice from behind him.

He wheeled. "Good-evening," he said, startled.

A pair of hazel-brown eyes smiled from a classically shaped face.

"You look surprised," she remarked.

"I am," he admitted. "Are you a visitor here?"

"I'm one of the dig." She sat easily on the arm of a carved oaken chair. Her red velvet dress charged the hall with vivid brilliance, culling his eye for effect, for colour superimposed on colour.

"I thought you existed in denims and shirts. Padraig's remarks were not complimentary."

"The rest of them do but I'm the Professor's secretary."

"I'm glad to hear," said Diarmid with relief, "that somebody is civilised. I was beginning to doubt."

"He does hate us, poor darling."

"If he loathes you so much, why does he allow you to trample his precious turf and prod his green pastures?"

"He's interested really."

He felt she knew more about Padraig than he did. "I'm ignorant about it. He and I haven't met for several years except for a few minutes in the war."

"You're his brother?" suddenly.

He nodded. "Didn't he say I was coming? He tore you all to pieces in the letter.

I was to come to save him from the influx."

"That's his peculiar amusement," said the girl. "After a day or two, you'll see."

"I'm just beginning to wonder if I'll stay."

"Oh, you must. We are progressing remarkably well. The Professor is more than gratified with the results so far. You must come down and see for yourself."

"If you have an Irish room, I will."

"An Irish room?" She wrinkled her brow. "We have two yards of ancient wall."

"That's the name of the play I've brought with me. By Conal O'Bridie."

"He lives in my father's house," was her next astonishing remark.

"Your father's house?" He blinked and began to quote irreverently: " '*In my Father's house are many mansions . . .*' It seems like that. Hector's landlord, you mean? I was given to understand he was Sir Bruno Waldstein . . ."

"My father. At least, he adopted me when I lost my own parents. They were his greatest friends. Like you," she added gently, "I am an orphan."

He began to see. He had heard much of Sir Bruno Waldstein, a man famed in City finance, a director of countless companies, an owner of much property, soon, it was rumoured, to be Lord Mayor of London.

"He's very proud," she went on. "It is an honour he has long craved. He will make a fine Lord Mayor."

"I am sure he will." Sir Bruno made a success of everything he touched. He had certainly made a success of his adopted daughter. "How strange that there should be a link between us, through Hector. You know Hector? — "

"Not personally. I insisted on earning my living," with a playful smile curving round the corners of her eyes. "Father was chagrined but he recognised the spirit behind the choice. That is where he excels above the ordinary parent."

"He sounds remarkable."

"I'd like to meet Mr. Burne," she continued. "I understood he received few visitors."

"He receives rarely and commands regally." His lips creased. "I was on my way to the station when he sent for me. He must think Ireland an ineluctable place."

"He uses an Irish pseudonym."

"A great-grandfather who died at Sebastopol. Or is my history askew? Anyway, no more close than that."

"An Irish room has something to do with the play?"

"Everything, I anticipate. So far I've only got as far as the title and the *dramatis personae*. An odd set of characters plunged into some crisis. Hector excels in that type of setting though previously he has chosen more orthodox *locales*. However, we haven't as yet introduced ourselves seeing that you are in the west wing and I am in the east wing and Padraig presumably dwells in between. My name is Diarmid, after that cavalier yonder. He resisted the butcher Cromwell to the death."

She followed his gaze to where a dark, almost undecipherable painting hung in a corner. The only part which held the eye was a wide collar of embroidered lace.

"A fancy fellow," she mused lightly. "I'm beginning to place you. I did hear of a Venetian palace being created in Milsom Street. Father was at the opening and wrote me a screed. I was in Corfu at the time, with a team investigating a pre-Crusadic temple."

"Otherwise you might have been there."

He matched his tone to hers. "That was a task Lewis gave me. The old chap was bemused by those paintings of Braydon's. They were certainly good and out of it he found Mora. Tell me, didn't Sir Bruno buy a couple?"

"He did; exquisite, they are. He gave me one, of the Palazzo Verdoni in the cool of the evening. I've never been to Venice. Always, when Father goes I'm at the other end of the world. It's my penalty, he says, for preferring to work."

He laughed. "Next to Venice itself I'd say the best substitute is a Braydon painting. Mine is a corner of the Piazzo San Mateo, a perfect gem. It hangs in my studio and gives me inspiration in my 'dead' moments."

"You have done well, haven't you? Mr. Riall is slightly jealous. He reads about you in the papers."

"He needn't be. He has Marchmont."

"You'd like it?"

"Not really, not for ever, but . . ."

"It's in you; it's a part of you; you've wanted to come, to satisfy yourself you can do without it. Is that it?"

"What are you?" he enquired. "A

clairvoyant, along with the other magicians ? Ancient walls, witches on broomsticks, tiny leprechauns. Aunt Ma-Ma would have frowned on my chatterings."

"Who was Aunt Ma-Ma ?"

"The one who brought me up."

"Nice ?"

"Hardly. Conscientious, puritanical, card-playing, without humour, without beauty."

"Diarmid!"

"She did her best," he allowed. "I owe her my education and the beginning of my career. Her house was so awful I spent my leisure hours replanning it."

"Why did you never come to Marchmont before ?"

"Padraig never asked me."

She paused; then: "I see."

A man was coming down the stairs, white-haired and frail, his eyesight frail too from the way he peered forward, his shoulders bent, his crushed and creased suit hanging limply from his body. It needed no special percipience to guess that this was Alec Codrill.

"Ah, Marcia!"

"Professor, this is Diarmid Riall, Mr.

Riall's brother. He has come to stay at Marchmont for a few days."

Codrill advanced across the stone floor. "You'll be in time for the discovery," he said at once.

"I had hoped so," replied Diarmid. Over the white head, he gave Marcia — the right, the only, the most satisfying name for her! — a tender twinkle. "Padraig wrote you were on the eve of a great find. I know little about digs though when the temple of Mithros was opened in the City I went there every day."

He was designing a Greek backcloth and the findings of the experts had added to his researches at the British Museum and the Victoria and Albert Museum.

"That," said the Professor, "was a highly significant and exciting discovery, only comparable to the finding of the Apollo remains in Cethos. You remember them?"

"Not so clearly. When was that, Professor?"

"1946," said Marcia.

"Yes. 1946."

"I was in the RAF," said Diarmid, "doing my service in Burma, far removed, I'm afraid, from Greek soil."

"Burma! What a pity I didn't know. You could have investigated the great Pegu pagoda where it is rumoured Queen Sawbu hid the dynastic jewels."

"Hardly in RAF uniform but," placatingly, anticipating the full flood of a lover in need of an audience, "you must tell me another time. Here comes Padraig to tell us dinner is served."

"Sherry is in the library, Professor." The owner of Marchmont was in full evening dress and moved with the ease and dignity of a man in possession. An old jingle echoed inanely in Diarmid's mind. *"When Riall of Marchmont Royal went riding . . ."* No, the next verse. *"When Riall of Marchmont Royal went drinking . . ."* Sherry before dinner was hardly drinking. He was fey and outside himself, the culmination of many hours of travelling and new surroundings, not the least this fresh-featured girl who was related to Sir Bruno Waldstein.

"Delighted," said Alec Codrill and hurried short-sightedly after Padraig.

"Is he really like that," asked Diarmid, "or is it a pose?"

"He exaggerates," smiled Marcia, "when

he has an audience. He's like all the men. He loves to be on show."

"I think that's a little cruel." The soft amused laugh was still in his ear, like a muted string on a windless night, or an echo across a low pasture.

"Life is cruel, isn't it?" she said and he followed her to the library with a host of unformulated queries chasing in his mind.

3

LIFE is cruel. It seemed an odd thing for a girl to say, a girl as fortunate and self-possessed as Marcia French. He learned her surname when Padraig, extricating himself from Professor Codrill's account of the day's dig, turned to her with an almost desperate eagerness. "More chicken, Miss French?" She had been about to refuse; then swiftly, almost apologetically, Diarmid thought, accepted and held her plate for Brigid to refill. Across the space between, their eyes met and there was some message in hers he could not read, though he guessed it was referring to Padraig. In a vague way, she seemed to be excusing his brother, making allowances for him, though he could not for the life of him explain why. To him, it appeared that Padraig was cushioned from the chatter and malice of the world, secreted in this western corner of civilisation, answerable only to his conscience and the wind and the rain. Was there some problem? He glanced at Padraig at the head of the table, once more receiving the full output of the Professor's thin, continuous treble, and tried to assess the character behind the pinched-in forehead. It was useless. He knew little or nothing of Padraig and until he did he could not pretend to judge or disparage.

The rest of the dig were lodged in the bothy, surrounding the rear courtyard. Only Codrill and Marcia slept in the house, eating with the owner. For that he could be grateful, for it would enliven his evenings and enable him to study the situation. Suddenly, he longed for Hector, to analyse this disputable household with his clinical brain, seeing in it possibilities for a play. He would write him and tell him he had a ready-made plot. There was no need of Lady Luke and her pansy son, Father Flaherty, Superintendent Boyle, or even the urchin Tim. An abstracted bachelor landowner, a professor of archaeology, a secretary and a brother from England, Mrs. Sullivan to lend variety and Brigid to drop soft Gaelic mouthings into the cumulative tide of exposition. Outside, a mob of diggers turning up the sacred, unspoiled earth.

"A penny for them," Marcia said across the table.

"They're worth more than a penny. I was writing a synopsis for Hector."

"With us — ?"

"With us," he replied. "Don't you think there are possibilities?"

"Too many." She surprised him and he was again aware of cross purposes . . . but when next he glanced at her she was smiling and the mere suggestion of drama was anachronistic. The Professor talked on; Padraig fingered the stem of his wine glass; Brigid had withdrawn; and a glow, golden and luminous, came in through the windows from behind the Reek. He was tired and the insertive magic of Marchmont that Aunt Ma-Ma had striven against so strenuously, guarding him like a lioness her cub, had mingled with the bounty of the wine and caused him to float in a sea of hazard and imaginings.

"You must come down tomorrow," said Marcia, "to see our progress."

"I will, of course."

"You're not angry because we are finding treasures?"

"Are you finding treasures? Padraig said . . ."

"We have found the walls of an abbey. The Professor is telling your brother his theory of the order."

"Tell me," he invited.

"I'm not so learned as the Professor."

"Don't you type his notes?"

"Yes. He thinks there was an abbey here in AD 680."

"Cuimin was on Clunare from AD 520, when he landed until 561 when he was murdered by Tiernan. He established his church and the day my mother was drowned she had taken her cousin to see it. They stayed too long and got caught in a storm which blew up from the west. We haven't much faith in St. Cuimin. He didn't save his worshippers."

"Wasn't it their fault for staying too long? They had been warned about the tides. I'm sorry," she said slowly. "I've been here long enough to have heard the story a dozen times. Every villager for miles around knows your mother went to Clunare on a day of high tide when the wind was against the land and went in defiance of your father, moreover."

"You must implement the gaps in my knowledge."

"I thought you knew. Everybody here seems to know."

"Aunt Ma-Ma was not fond of my father. I scent a forbidden alliance. Or is that my romanticism coming to the fore?"

"The facts about St. Cuimin are few and scarce. He landed on Clunare in 520, and built a church there. The remains can be seen."

"I'm relieved."

She ignored his retort. Her voice was warm and pleasant like a cloudless sky in the bay. "He gathered about him a community of fellow Christians and in 554 he began to build an abbey on the mainland."

"I've never heard that," said Diarmid.

"It's safe to assume that Quilty's Pasture was the site selected by the saint. It was within reach of Clunare, across the bay, in the shelter of the Reek and the Pins, an ideal spot for a contemplative order."

"Except for the lowness of the soil. Wasn't St. Cuimin a militant saint? I remember my nurse telling me tales of his priesthood. The stories had been handed down through the generations."

"Yes," agreed Marcia. "That's true but in the new abbey the community would have a base; it would settle there and begin the services and the acts that became part of the Christian religion as it established itself in the northern hemisphere. A saint of Cuimin's stature would look far beyond the initial struggling necessary to build his church. As Rialls in later years fought and settled at Marchmont, so Cuimin in 554 foresaw long centuries of Christian worship in a place worthy of the sacrifice of the Master. The abbey was a tremendous undertaking, not finished in his lifetime. Cedricus Adrianus, Cuthbertus, all added to his inspiration and caused the vast building to be erected."

"You've found remains?"

"Not yet. We've hardly had time. We've only been here a couple of months. We need many more. It's a painstaking job, sifting the tiny crumbs of evidence, examining the earth and stones we find, but we are confident of success."

"Don't you have failures?"

"Many," replied Marcia, "or such minute particles of proof as to be almost non-existent."

49

"Then what — ?" he began.

"Take a look at the Professor. Would you say he was a disconsolate man?"

"On the contrary, he grows more ebullient every moment. Since he has been at the table, he has changed materially. Padraig is bemused by his erudition."

"He is a clever man. When he is convinced of a point, it would take more than a landed Irishman to move him."

"That I can well believe." Yet Codrill in appearance was the opposite of convincing. A chatterer, a charlatan strutting a minor stage, sporting a formula invented over the years. Diarmid had seen and heard many. There had been a man at St. Withburga's, the living spit of the Professor, who deluded the authorities for a decade and was finally caught by a chance in a hundred. "Who could doubt a man whose choice of subject is far remote from the realms of ordinary men?"

"You laugh at him?"

"Perhaps. Is it important to disinter St. Cuimin from his grave? It is vital to know whether he lived here or yonder fourteen-hundred years ago?"

"To the Professor it is. He'd die without

his stones and his bones. You mustn't laugh at him," sharply. "To every man his loves and his likes. Whereas my father is happy with money, the Professor must dig. You make designs with paint and marble; I type and decipher ancient documents; others teach and mine coal and repair motor cars. I wouldn't say any of them were unnecessary. It's good to be employed, however inanely in other people's eyes."

"You class us all in unproductive trades?"

"No," smiled Marcia. "A collector of paintings is preserving for the future great masterpieces of the past; tattered, musty volumes may contain a wisdom without price if the volumes can be found and taken care of. Is it not a matter of the drones and the queens? Without the drones the hive would be sterile but without the queens the drones would not work. Beauty and culture and art and history may not mine coal or drive milk lorries but they are vital to civilisation, for the cultivation of men's minds. In the abbey of St. Cuimin, men spent decades illuminating scriptures or composing for their and other people's spiritual comfort volumes of priceless value. To find only one of such a volume would repay for all time the energy and the toil expended on the searching."

"I begin to understand," thoughtfully, "that you are a devout disciple and I must mind my p's and q's."

"I don't need to say such things to you. You deal in beauty and beautiful things."

"With drones and butterflies," honestly. He saw why she had insisted on going her own way, despite the wish of Sir Bruno to restrain her.

"They are the means. The culmination of the effort, surely, is the crowning glory."

"Which you find in old stones?"

"In the finding of priceless treasures," she corrected.

"I hope then," said Diarmid, "you achieve success at Marchmont."

"Nevertheless, you are not convinced we are digging in the right spot?"

"I'll keep an open mind. I must pay a visit to Clunare and renew my acquaintance with Cuimin's church. If I remember correctly — I was only a small boy when I was here — it stands on a promontory over a spur of rocks. He must have been a grand builder."

"A man with my father's foresight."

At the other end of the table, Padraig was rising, saying: "It's all very interesting, Professor," with a harsh ring in his voice, as though he could accept little more without dislodging his temper. He had refilled his glass, Diarmid knew; his hollow, hungry face was blank and set. A man who was unhappy within himself? Och, and bitter? Diarmid glimpsed the acidity deep down in Padraig; a sourness with men or with nature?

"I haven't had chance yet to hear the Professor on Cuimin's Abbey. Miss French has been putting me in the picture. Do we adjourn?"

"You'll excuse me?" said Codrill. He had his napkin tucked into his shirt front. Diarmid removed it and placed it on the table. "I have the day's findings to tabulate."

"Are we losing Miss French?"

"If you'll excuse me," put in Marcia. "You must have much to say to each other." She smiled at Padraig. "We usually withdraw at the close of dinner. The Professor likes to make notes and decide any alteration of plan for the morrow. Good-night, Mr. Riall."

Padraig, granted the withdrawal. "Good-night, Miss French."

"Good-night," to Diarmid.

He half-protested; then said: "Good-night, Miss French. May I come down in the morning, Professor? I'm very interested."

"Do."

Padraig invited: "Come into the smoking-room," and led the way, across the hall, beneath the dirty portraits.

"You need lightening in here. All this old oak needs stripping, the walls baring. I'd forgotten the Royal was so dark. It's like a morgue."

"It suits me," Padraig stated.

"Faith," said Diarmid, "there's no need to bury yourself alive! What do you do here?"

"There are sheep."

"Nothing else. Did our father leave you comfortable?" His eyes glinted with amusement. The smoking-room walls were four feet thick, as were the walls of

54

most of the house. Padraig's theory that this had been Cuimin's abbey had a faint glimmer of reason. He touched the stone window ledge. "What was this? The abbot's pantry?"

The other paused in the act of pouring two glasses of whisky.

"I'm not in the mood for banter, Diarmid."

"I meant it," he replied. "Why build an abbey in Quilty's Pasture when this was here?"

"You're reacting already to the pratings of that fool."

"I caught little of his discourse. He mumbled a lot and Marcia French was enlightening."

"She's attractive, I agree."

"Sir Bruno Waldstein's adopted daughter, she told me. Do you realise what that means?"

"I assume you know the man."

"I know of him." Diarmid settled himself into one of the leather-studded chairs. "It's impossible not to if you are resident in London. Any national appeal finds his name at the top. He's landlord to thousands in the City and in the West End. He owns

Waddesdon Square where Hector Burne lives. With his patronage — "

"You've only to enlist Miss French's assistance . . ."

"That wouldn't be as easy as it sounds." He met Padraig's darkening glance. "An attractive person but hard set against the exploiters. I imagine she fancies herself as Codrill's lieutenant. Nevertheless, I like her. I found her easy to talk to, if veering on the side of ancient history. I must browse in the library while I am here. There should be books amongst that vast collection which will tell me something of the period."

"Many. I have added a half hundred in recent years."

"You . . . Padraig, you old hermit! I didn't know you were a scholar of antiquity. Come on. Let me into the picture. Tell me everything since we were swept away on that night of wind and rain. I always associated Marchmont with wind. It's one reason why I've never attempted to exert myself. There must be something of the same proclivity in both of us. Each sitting in our own acre. Do you have to be dragged from your magnifying glass as I have to be dragged from my work table?"

"You have a right to know, I presume."

"I should think I have. I submit myself to a long journey by train and sea and arrive here finally at the edge of beyond in answer to the cry of distress you sent me. You appeared to be master of the madman at dinner."

"He was somewhat subdued this evening. Your presence, I should say."

"Tell that to Lewis!" cried Diarmid. "If that is a subdued mood, what is an exhilarated one? Didn't they find a new stone?"

"You'll find out soon enough. I wish I had never allowed them to come. In a weak moment, I agreed to the request, thinking it would prove interesting to a certain piece of research I had been asked to do for Cuimin's College in Dunphilly. It was the Master who asked if Alec Codrill might come. He had a theory concerning St. Cuimin which affected the college. My scholarship was well-known and in Cloncobh, you know, Cuimin is regarded with particular reverence. Each year there is a pilgrimage to Clunare, to his church, and daily some poor fool asks to cross to his shrine to cure his rheumatics or his ailments. I was not enamoured of the thought of hordes of foreigners swarming over Marchmont but the Master persisted. Codrill was a dedicated man, eager to pursue his latest theory, and the resultant fame and discoveries would benefit all. If it could be proved that Cuimin had an abbey in Quilty's Pasture, the seat of the shrine could be assumed to have been there and the dangerous crossing of the bay and its record of sad tragedies could be removed. I can guess your retort. If Cuimin's church on the island has the holy powers, how would the finding of another lessen their importance? It would not, to the students and believers, but it would save the wicked crossing at all times of the year and keep the actual shrine unmolested and perpetual."

"I'm a bit in the dark, Padraig. Do people cross to the island to petition the saint?"

"Every week. Strangely enough, in recent years, the habit has increased. Since Kirsty O'Halloran had the cancer and was rowed across on a wild October night and came back in the morning a new woman. Literally, a new woman. You'd be aware, Diarmid, if you had seen her, wasted and skin and bone, on the verge of receiving absolution."

"I knew miracles did happen." He sipped his whisky reflectively. Was Padraig mystic, bending his will to ancient rites? Why had he sent for him? Because of the dig, or the onset of loneliness, or the definite desire to learn more of his distant brother? A fight to preserve a holy shrine?

Naturally, he was superstitious. He had lived alone at the Royal, with only Mrs. Sullivan and Brigid Malone to feed his thoughts. In this violation of Marchmont's soil he saw an attempt to depose him from its tenancy. Maybe.

He shivered and wished Marcia French had been with them, or even Aunt Ma-Ma, arch enemy of all Rialls. She would have put up with no nonsense.

"We must halt these suicidal trips," went on Padraig. "Superintendent Mulligan came to see me. He appealed to me to use my influence. Clunare belongs to me. Would I cut it off?"

"Has it ever been cut off?"

"It has never been cut off. Not even after our mother died. In his desolation Father went often to the shrine, to lay his grief on the broken altar. Uncle Patrick told me, after a visit here, and it was confirmed by Mrs. Sullivan when I returned."

"Surely, to cut it off would make it more precious," reasoned Diarmid.

"That was my contention."

"So when you were asked to agree to a dig . . ."

"You see its possibilities?"

"Will the locals accept a new shrine?"

"If they are educated," sternly. "The rural Irish are credulous and fancy-ridden. They have followed the Rialls for three generations."

"They'll follow you?"

"Why should they not?"

"I couldn't say. I haven't been here long enough. You'll have to let me poke around; that is, if you want my assistance."

"I'd value your opinion, Diarmid."

It was a concession which Diarmid grasped eagerly, repeating his plea for a history of Padraig's early years.

" 'Twas lonely I was," eventually said Padraig, emptying his glass and sitting back in his chair, "without our mother or yourself, cooped up in that urban house of Uncle Patrick, with no hills to climb, no horses to ride. He was nothing like our father. A dried-up stick of a man, his nose in his ledgers, going every morning to his office in Carnford Street and every evening shutting himself in his room and counting his customers. A tradesman, Uncle Patrick, not one to relish a small boy, bruised and aching for a loss."

"He sounds as exacting as Aunt Ma-Ma. I took a refuge in drawing."

"I found the Mallinbray Library and wore out a stool in its reference room," with a shy glint of retarded humour. "Aunt Clara was always complaining that I had no seat in my pants. I wriggled so on the stool I went through the new seats she gave me. She never had any money from our father for my suits."

"She should have been like Aunt Ma-Ma and pestered him. I had my education paid by Riall money."

"I found the accounts when I came home. Five hundred pounds our father sent to Aunt Maisie for your education. I had to work for my scholarships."

"In faith! You mean he never paid a penny? You should have come — "

"I did," with a dry grimness. "When I

was through Grammar School and wanted to go to Trinity and Uncle Patrick said I should come home; there was no reason why I should stay on. I'd gone there when Mother was drowned and Father prostrate with grief. So I packed my cases and came here and Father said: 'Who are you?' I said: 'Padraig. Haven't you a welcome for me?' 'Indeed, I have not', he shouted. 'I have no welcome for anybody'. Queer, he was, Diarmid, looking at me with a fierce light in his eyes and treating me as though I was a stranger. I spent that night and subsequent ones at Kirsty O'Halloran's and the stories she told me of the Royal and our father were not nice for an eighteen-year-old's mind. 'I'd go back to Glenmoy', she said and when I said I hadn't any money, Uncle Patrick had sent me home, she countered: 'Well, you can earn some, Padraig Riall. Can't you go for a teacher? Have you learned nothing with that stuffed shirt of a tradesman? Can you no turn your hand to anything? A fine owner of March-mont you'll be when the time comes'. Scornful, she was, like rust, itching me. That was before she was taken with the cancer. Fine, she was, and upstanding. A prideful woman, and I a callow youth, but I said: 'I'll go for a teacher, Kirsty, if you'll come with me'. 'Faith Diarmid you wouldn't know my loneliness! The hurt of it when our father said: 'Who are you?' His own son and he would not know him. Kirsty was blunt-spoken. 'There's kind for you, Padraig Riall. Mind you never do the same to yours'," and a shadow was over his features.

"She'd not approve your silence all these years," remarked Diarmid.

"She does not approve many things I've done," Padraig said heavily.

"You took her?"

"I took her," he complied. "I was eighteen and she twenty-four. I was a boy and she a woman. I was a Riall and she an O'Halloran. I was hurt and bitter and sore and betrayed. I'd show our father, I said, and Kirsty encouraged me. Let him come and part us, she said; she'd tell him a few hometruths. But he never did. He never gave a sign whether he knew or not. After I returned, I knew he had, but he'd let me go, wiped me out of his life as he wiped you. An odd man, our father, not the same as other men."

"He lost more than a wife when Mother died. Aunt Ma-Ma said she was a jewel of his crown, that so long as she was here he would listen. To her but not to anybody else. I suppose he lost hold of everything. I'm sorry for him, Padraig. This lovely spot and no one to share it with him."

"He shouldn't have sent us away. I could have been his companion. As it was, I had Kirsty, a poor substitute." The bitterness was all too apparent. "I soon found what I had done. I had exchanged Uncle Patrick and Aunt Clara for a further shackle."

Diarmid was quiet. He could feel the tragedy of that far-off act, the hurt youth offering himself to the first woman who spoke kindly to him.

"We had rooms in O'Logan Street. I found a job in an infants' school and she took employment with a Mrs. Shane. I hated the life and would have left it but for her violent, scabrous tongue. 'You a Riall,' she would say. 'You're like the rest of that ruinous bunch. What's teaching a few kids?' Begorra!" he cried. "I could have throttled her but I needed her. In my misery and my loneliness, I needed her. Somehow I must earn the money to go to university; how better than by double wage packets? So we stayed until the April when I went home one evening and found a note saying she'd gone to England with Mrs. Shane. The choice we'd made had not been a wise one. I should find myself a comfortable studious job so that when my father died and I inherited the Royal I could return. She did not suppose she would ever go back to Cloncobh."

"You said she went to Clunare when she was ill."

"She did and gave me a miracle to add to the other benefits."

"I can see you are bitter. You acted thoughtlessly and selfishly."

"I was a youth with no roots."

"You had the inheritance. You should have stood up to our father, told him to reassert himself, tackle his responsibilities."

"You cannot judge," harshly. "You weren't here. My initiative had been sapped with Uncle Patrick."

Was Padraig a weakling? Diarmid experienced a rush of revulsion.

"A pity you weren't sent to Aunt Ma-

Ma. A dose of that Victorian household would have stiffened you," tersely. He was disgusted at the revelation. "And Kirsty? Did you never try to repay her what she did for you? Had she to wait until she was dying of the cancer and you turned the other cheek? For shame, Padraig Riall," stung by the consequences he conjured from the pitiful, self-conscious betrayal. "You let her be rowed across the bay on a storm-lashed night and now you begrudge her the miracle she found and would take the shrine away because she lives and you wanted her to die. Is that it?"

Begod, he was in the midst of a drama here! He was sitting forward in his chair, flashing angrily at his brother, flinging his tones at the dark, shadowed figure, all the normal sparkle and light wiped from his features.

"She shamed you in those youthful days. She showed you the man you were not. No wonder we never saw you, we never heard a word from you. Uncle Patrick cut you off; Aunt Clara would not speak to you, taking Kirsty O'Halloran and letting her go . . ."

"She went herself," furiously.

"You never stopped her. You made no attempt to hold her. Would she have gone with Mrs. Shane if she had been contented with you? There must have been some encouragement. You were no ignorant boy, falling for a country wench. You were Ruaidhri Riall's son, bitter with your position, raging with injured pride. You'd show them; you'd prove to Cloncobh and the rest of the world you were no pup. I remember occasions when we were boys. No, Padraig, I'm not ignorant. You treated Kirsty like muck and a long time after your sin found you out."

The smoking-room was charged with gall. Padraig was sunk in his chair, brooding, grey, older than his actual years. Opposite him, Diarmid's dark brown eyes held contempt and denunciation.

"It was time I came," clearly, "to see Kirsty O'Halloran . . ."

"You will not — "

". . . to find what manner of man lives at Marchmont . . ."

"I have suffered," said Padraig.

"As you deserve to suffer," promptly. "To turn a woman away whom once you had taken — "

67

"I never said — "

"That is what you did. I have the sight, they always said. My mother, in our bedroom at night, bending over my bed, shy and afraid: 'You have the sight, Diarmid.' I never needed it before. In Aunt Ma-Ma's house, all was above board, save when Victor had his final fling. I must tell you about that. A dark horse, Uncle Victor, but clear dark. Not muddy-dark, as you were. Does Ruaidhri know the son he bore?"

"I'll not have you — " frenziedly.

"You cannot tell so much and not all. You cannot appeal and turn me out within twenty-four hours. You need me, is that not so? You have got yourself in a bog, as I recollect Mickey Nolan once did, up to his armpits, and Father strode across the tufts and lifted him out and rated him for his foolishness. 'Is it quite blind you are, man, to come across Kilmeenan in the dusklight?' Is it quite blind you are, Padraig, to send for me and turn the other eye?"

Finally: "I'm bludgeoned and beset by these diggers."

"Whom you allowed to come. Back to Kirsty. You can't discount a miracle,

68

Padraig. Kirsty was sick and was made well. Who saw her at death's door?"

"Father O'Rourke, Doctor Costain, the neighbours."

"Who carried her to Clunare?"

"Another O'Halloran."

"Were there witnesses?"

"God's truth," swore Padraig hotly, "I saw her, coming ashore at the first light, hale and well."

"What did you do?" relentlessly.

"I hid my eyes."

"As shame must force you to do. Did you speak?"

"She said: 'Padraig, I am whole. God has been good and kind. He has forgiven — .'"

"Forgiven?"

"The sin we shared. Diarmid, I'll not answer you, begorra. I'll only answer to God — "

"Did you not answer to God then, on the shore of Cloncobh, when Kirsty stood before you?"

"I told her," bowing his head, "I would have nothing to do with it. I had finished with her when she left me . . ."

"Did she never tell you why she left?"

"It was in the letter," briefly. "She did not want to be a drag. I want nothing to do with her or with him. I never thought to confess, on your first night at the Royal, but you wanted an account, you forced me to tell you — "

"Indeed, Padraig, you wanted to tell me. You've had this sore running for years. You should have had me earlier. Why do we have relations if not to seek their solace when we are bedevilled? My friend Lewis has a friend, a Church of England priest, who would do you a world of good. He would, Padraig. An hour with Dudley Spence and you'd see things in a better perspective. Don't rear like a frightened horse! You've been sitting here, brooding . . ."

"Kirsty was real, is real," stated Padraig.

"What happened after that? You came to Victoria Road on your way to embark."

"I was sent to Salerno. We tramped the long road to Cassino and beyond. I was sickened with death and wounding and shelling and with war. I kept going by remembering this place. It was a green oasis."

"You found no companionship?"

"I was through with companionship," harshly. "I trusted no man." He might have added: No woman either. "At Valmonte a man came to see me. He said his name was McMaughan. He was the son of the gardener here, though I had not known him. My father was dead, he said. He had heard from his family. The Royal was awaiting its new master. Then, strangely I revolted against it. I did not want its refuge. I thought: Kirsty came from Cloncobh. The sin will be with me. So I held back, for a long time, until I saw an advertisement in the paper, asking if I were dead, and I couldn't bear for them to dispose of me and install you in my place."

"What an odd creature you are," commented Diarmid. "I can't imagine anyone not wanting Marchmont."

"It's riddled with debts, rotten with woodworm, eaten up with jealousies, given over to the little people, occupied by diggers. If I could get out, I would. I'd go to Dublin and apply for a tutorship. I've passed my exams. There's nothing else to do here but study and browse and stare at the sea. I've catalogued the library. You'd be surprised at the value. But it's entailed. The whole estate is entailed — and I have no son."

Diarmid half-opened his mouth; then saw the refusal in the dark, bitter eyes.

"I'm caught, as our father was caught. No wonder he ended the talk of the countryside."

"There must be some way. Lease it to a school, a college, an old people's home. Find a rich American to restore it and live in it while you're away to the college. There's no need to stagnate. Have a career. You're clever. You're wasted down here."

"I'm caught," repeated Padraig. He poured himself another glass of whisky. "When you've been here a little longer, you'll see."

"Nobody's caught," decidedly, "unless he wishes to be." Was that it? Did Padraig enjoy his martyrdom, self-inflicted to bury his guilty conscience? Quite obviously, a visit to Kirsty was indicated. And to Clunare. There he might find the antidote to this malaise that had Padraig in thrall.

A clever chap? He wondered wordlessly. That short visit many years before had given them no clue to the actual man. An easy speech, a body covered by the khaki uniform gave no hint of troubled moments and restless shame. The old chap was making too much of it. Scores of fellows did what he had done and thought no more of it After all, it had been six of one and half dozen of the other. A weak boy and a thrustful woman. Six years on the wrong side. Another page in Riall history.

It was the whisky clouding their judgments. And his long journey from London. Tomorrow, he would see all this for the fanciful story it was. Padraig was leading him on, lending credence to his Irish credulity. When he got upstairs, he must put it on paper. A ready-made plot. Not *The Irish Room* but *The Isle of Clunare*. He pushed back his chair.

"I've had a long day. Will you excuse me? We must have some more talks. And I want to see Marchmont. This is a holiday, my first for years. I've had my nose to the grindstone, building up my business. I'll inspect the dig and make the acquaintance of the rest of the team; and go to Clunare. I want to see Cuimin's church. I always promised I would one day. And soak up the atmosphere, if I'm to design a set for

Hector's play. I've scarcely looked at it yet and he's some fascinating characters. You must read it and give me your opinion. Another view often clarifies the position. Hector will be pleased. He likes praise and you can't but like it. Don't disturb yourself," as he rose. "I can't find my way. So long as I don't go westwards and intrude on your guests." He smiled easily, turning towards the door. "We've had a long sitting. I should turn in yourself, if I were you. Everything looks fresher in the morning."

4

HE had much to think about but he was too weary, mentally and physically, to lie long awake. Somewhere in the distance he heard the roar of the sea, the treacherous breakers that came in from the west and swirled round the base of the rocks, but from his room in the eastern wing it was a languorous murmur; he was lulled by the sound. He only had time to think: I must get to the bottom of this uneasiness; then no more. In hardly any time at all, it seemed, it was morning and a shimmering golden sun was slanting into his room.

He sprang out of bed and flung wide the casement. The whole of the Reek was flooded with a vitreous light. The beauty, the breath-aching beauty of it, drawing the emotions, clutching the throat muscles! Rapidly, he pullled on his clothes and ran downstairs. A boy, paddling in the dew, turning to see his mother, a figure in blue . . .

There was a figure in blue; it was smiling

at his naked feet, his boyish enjoyment in this return to his home.

"I didn't think anybody was so un-inhibited . . ."

"It's delicious!"

"I always wanted to do it myself," smiled Marcia.

"Why not? There's nobody about. It's barely six o'clock. I was awake. I smelt the dew."

"Mr. Riall would think us mad."

With a glance at the old house: "Padraig may think what he likes. He has a poor opinion of the world so another demon-stration of its inanity will hardly cure his jaundice. Tell me," suddenly serious, "do you think Padraig a sick man?"

"I hardly know — " she began.

"I'm fey, I know. This is Ireland. This is Marchmont, where a set of madmen are digging for an old abbey. Across the bay is a holy island. Did you know that? Miracles have taken place. Though not for my mother."

"She was drowned. Mr. Riall told us."

"Padraig delights in adding to the gloom. He's not well, I'm afraid. We must be patient with him. But let me hold your shoes. And call me Diarmid. We can't have two Mr. Rialls. If we are to be companions — "

"I have work to do."

"Secretarial, professional. I have work as well. But not today. Not at this moment. This is magic. Once, at St. Withburga's, Lewis and I paddled in the dew. It's fun, Marcia," he said. "It gives the toes a glorious freedom, or light as air effect; it releases the spirit . . . I'm not demented," he smiled. "Actually, I'm not very happy about my brother. He's gone astray somewhere. You may be able to help. There's a long story and so far I only know a portion of it. Isn't it wonderful?" as she took off her stockings and put her toes to the grass. "Over this way," and led her through the garden, to the pasture beyond, to where the dig was taking place, the turf interspersed the heaps of earth and wells of excavation. "Admit that it's the only thing to do at Marchmont. There's no such thing as time and morality. Time doesn't count. This proves it."

"Diarmid — " She was laughing at him, shaking her head at him. "No wonder I hear tales of you in London."

"I wouldn't dare do this in London."

"That mad Irishman, Father said one day, turning drawing-rooms into coliseums."

"Northland House," said Diarmid. "I'm glad he saw it."

"I shall write him to commission you to do the Lord Mayor's show."

"I shall be delighted, and charge the earth."

"He'll pay," she promised.

"Because you say so?"

"No, because Diarmid Riall is *the* decorator in London, the man of the moment."

"I shouldn't really be on holiday," he said.

"If you hadn't come, I shouldn't have met you and I couldn't have written to Father as I'm going to do."

"I'm glad I came," he riposted.

The dig was an area of virgin pasture. Beyond, on all sides the healthy and smooth-sided hills came down to the luscious green tract where wild thyme and yellow ragwort grew in abundance. They sat on a rock projecting from the soil and dried their feet on their handkerchiefs and put on their shoes. Then they walked more seriously though not less indigenously towards the first upheaved soil. All round them was the freshness and the glitter of the morning. "Look!" cried Marcia, "through the mist". He followed her gaze and in the gap between the Reek and the Pins which protected the pile of Marchmont from the sea there rose, like a fairy hill, the "rath" or shape of Clunare, pinky diaphanous, blue and mauve and all the colours of the rainbow, subdued, the first resting place of Cuimin.

" 'Tis beautiful," breathed Diarmid in the lilt that ran off his lips in a trickle of awe. "Times without number I have come out here in the dawn, run away from my nursemaid, and played amongst these old stones, though never guessing they were in any way connected with Cuimin, but 'tis never like that I have seen it. Always it was veiled in mist, hidden from the naked eye. I see in it an omen, an omen of success. St. Cuimin must be lookng favourably on your dig, the dear, faithful saint that he was. Maybe the time of the Royal's sickness is near its end. Maybe Padraig, if we can prise him from this malaise, will live again a Riall of the Royal, a true son of Ruaidhri. You think me crazed?" he enquired. "Because I see an island rising from the mist, a holy island . . ."

"No," she said slowly. "Different, Diarmid, from what you were last evening, affected, caught up in some fantasy, some special spell."

"It's the Professor's fault," he replied. "Digging in the Pasture."

"You know you approve. The shine in your eye is proof of your approbation. Last night you were not prepared to say. You were tired from your journey, concerned about Padraig, wary of your welcome . . ."

"Never that," he exclaimed. "The old chap had sent for me. 'Come and rescue me', he wrote, 'from these fiends and madmen'."

"Will you?" she asked.

He was standing on the heap of earth by the side of the first excavation. Looking down he saw a few rough stones, a pointer or two of wood, a line of string. Hardly enough to prove that St. Cuimin came across from Clunaire and built an abbey.

"Until I've met the madmen, I cannot say, but it seems to me, in the light of the morning, unhampered by Dunphilly whisky," with a quirk, "that his madmen might be other than your diggers. In his sad and sorry state — occasioned, I might add, by experience in his youth — he has apportioned the blame for his unhealthiness on what is mortal and not what is spritual. There is a streak in our family that clings to the supernatural, the island myths. Our father was a very superstitious man. Padraig is adrift in a curragh on a sea of conjecture and we must aid him, if we can. The glimpse of Clunare gives me hope that we may be able to find a way."

"I thought when I first came how intently he watched us, coming up behind us, acting unusually— Diarmid, do you mind me saying this?"

"Of course I don't. I hope you'll be an ally. In parts like this, small phantoms grow out of all proportion. He is besotted with an idea that he failed a certain Kirsty O'Halloran. Have you heard of her while you've been here?"

"Indeed, yes. One can hardly go into Dunphilly without knowing about her.

Kirsty O'Halloran is a special person, Diarmid. You'll love her."

"I fear once that Padraig loved her or if he did not she loved Padraig and the devil entered their abode and poisoned it. But I'm filling you up with *my* phantoms."

"I hope I can be of use," she replied.

"Tell me," he harked back to Kirsty, "you have seen her? You have spoken to her? You say she is a special person. Would she see me?"

"She'd be delighted to see you, Diarmid."

"Is she small and thin? Padraig says she was dying."

"On Doctor Costain's word. Do you know Doctor Costain?"

"No," he replied. "Father O'Rourke as well . . ."

"Wait till you meet Father O'Rourke."

"Marcia, are you telling me this miracle never happened?"

"Irishmen need miracles, is that it? You were held by Padraig's recital. I'm not saying he and they are not right. I'm only saying wait until you've seen the witnesses. Form your own conclusion. I'm open-minded, Diarmid, as are most of my generation. Miracles can happen. There were many during the war. I wouldn't question Kirsty O'Halloran. I admire the faith that believes in such manifestations."

"Is your own faith not as high?" indicating the dig. "There's no proof that Cuimin . . ."

She gave him an appraising look. "Touché. I should be hard put to it to prove to a college of professors that Cuimin lived here — at the moment, but already there is the hint. See." She jumped down into the shallow trench. "Only two feet below ground the remains of wattle and hemp." Delicately, she handed him the decaying matter. "We know that in those days the saints built their huts of wattle. In secluded valleys, where the surrounding hills and passes protected the sites, they had their churches, their sacristies, their refectories, their guest chambers, their offices. Have you been to the great foundations in England? Fountains, Rievaulx, Jervaulx. Seen the various buildings? There are more of them left, having been built of stone and mortar. The layout, however, was similar; the pattern of the saints remained unchanged over the centuries. Prayer, study, manual labour. Obedience, chastity, poverty, humility. Can you not see them, dedicated men, slaving for the glory of God, planting in the chosen soil the precious seed of Christianity? I like to sit here and visualise them, men of humble origin, working and praying, giving of themselves that in the years to come other men might see the light. That is what Marchmont has done for me. Before it was the triumph of discovery; now it is the reason for the doing. You are right. Marchmont has a power to affect us, whether for good or for evil rests with our natures. It has known great things and great men; it nurtured the holiest of men, the great saint himself of whom it was written 'served God and man and died content'. What a beautiful epitaph, Diarmid! If half the world could say that of itself, there would be no cause for shrill panic. Who, in this steel age, can honestly say he was aware..."

"I dare say Cuimin was not aware. He had his problems. Springs dried up; men were lost; curraghs capsized; brothers defaulted. The lust of the flesh warred with the desire of the spirit. It's a nice story, Marcia; we can lull ourselves by believing it; but in actual fact, in lives such as Padraig's — sorry, I'm worried about him — the temptations outweigh the chances. I'll see Doctor Costain and Father O'Rourke and have a talk with Mrs. Sullivan. She's here, in the house, cooking for him, implementing his wishes. A good, motherly soul, I'd call her, not addicted to the fairies."

"You and your fairies! If you want to see more, time's going despite your Irish contention that it stands still. It's a quarter to seven and the Professor rises at seven. The team will be arriving."

"I'll take your word for it. We've had a pleasant hour," replied Diarmid.

Padraig was in the morning-room.

"I've been out for a ramble. It was such a perfect morning."

"We have good mornings at March-mont. Later, it'll rain. The clouds are low over Clunare."

"Earlier on, it rose from the sea on a carpet of mist."

"You saw it?"

"Like a jewel in a cushion of silver."

"Only the fortunate see Clunare in its framework of hills." There was a hint of jealousy in the tone.

"Have you never seen it? Always, when I was a boy, it was wreathed in mist."

"Our mother saw it the day she died," hollowly.

"Begorra, are you suggesting . . ."

"She wanted to die."

"She — " Diarmid flung round, his eyes filled with bewilderment.

"She went there to die," continued Padraig. "If you don't believe it read her journal."

"Did she leave a journal? I thought she took Cousin Colum to visit the island and a storm came up and the boat was lost."

"Facts so far as they go."

"For heavens' sake, don't wrap everything in mystery! You're making yourself ill. If there's something you fear, if you've got yourself into a mess . . ."

"Not psychiatrists," shrilly. "They meddle and probe and make things a thousand times worse. Uncle Patrick sent for one when I was sixteen."

"I'd no idea. I'm sorry. Tell me about Mother. I find it hard to believe she wanted to die. One doesn't seek death at twenty-eight."

"When one is sickened of one's circumstances and living in fear of one's husband . . . Colum knew," said Padraig.

"What had he to do with it? He was merely visiting here, as he did during the summer months. You're extraordinarily good at working up omens. Instead of immersing yourself in the past, you should be weaving fairy tales for your children."

"You see fit to romanticise," sharply.

"Going back to our mother — how we digress!" Diarmid said. "You'll be telling me next Cousin Colum was in love with her and completed a suicide pact so that on the return from Clunare he upset the boat and they were drowned."

"No facts are on record."

"I'll not believe it. Can I read her journal?" he asked.

"She had contracted an incurable disease."

An unhappiness was invading the room, overcasting a love that had begun with such high hopes. "She went, a fairy of a

girl, to that harsh Riall of a man" —
Aunt Ma-Ma, when she was angered by
him and wished to denounce him. "She
went to her death." In all faith, he had
never grasped the edge of her cutting
remarks until now.

"She would have been a cripple and that
she could not bear."

The figure in blue was lightly etched
on memory, coming across the grass in
the sparkling dew, skimming the ground,
to gather him up and sing lilting tunes to
him, calling him a wicked one, saying he
would suffer from rheumatism before he
was of age. That dear, light, feathery
person a cripple? No wonder she fled to
Cuimin. Might she not have said, in the
moment of the shock: "I'd rather die."

"I never knew. It seems there are many
things I never knew. I'll prowl around,
renewing my acquaintance."

"Father O'Rourke is coming."

"What are his reactions to the dig?"

"You'll see him with the rest, using a
spade. A man of contradictory emotions,"
remarked Padraig, "whom I find it difficult
to admire, a man eaten up with mundane
things."

Potatoes and chickens? How sensible of Father O'Rourke. Even Cuimin, the holy saint, must have had potatoes and chickens when he established his community.

He was taken by the Professor to be introduced to the team and to be initiated into the progress of the dig.

"I have already seen the wattle," as Alec Codrill hurried over the thick, lush grass, rather like a hen seeking for worms. "Miss French was my guide. You are fortunate, Professor, in having the services of such an excellent secretary."

"She keeps me in order," chuckled Codrill.

"She impresses me as a person of great integrity and unusual adaptability."

"A dear good person," said Codrill.

"You're achieving what you set out to do?"

"Ah! Wait! It is early days. We have uncovered the remains of wattle huts on the extreme edge of the settlement."

"Surely all building at that time was wattle and hemp."

"A great deal with common mud and

straw. Those early settlers used the materials to hand."

"The stone came later?" Diarmid glanced over his shoulder at the house. In the soft morning light, it could take on the form and substance of a religious house, planted firmly and lovingly on the slightly rising ground. Local stone from the blue and mauve hills within sight, carted by manual labour along the trodden routes, erected painstakingly and with faith. "You are not concerned then with a later community?"

"All Cuimin did concerns us," said the Professor. "We unearth and transcribe. Archaeology is a patient accumulation. A scrap here, months of sifting there, a portion of pottery, a chip of tile. You modern young men — "

"I admit I move with a faster speed," rejoined Diarmid. "Often I'm given only four weeks to erect my edifice."

"Unless we do this, civilisation will destroy the ancient arts. Everywhere you go modern building is obscuring the remains of the old. Chester, York, Sarum — we must move rapidly and plot and preserve and then all is filled in and above it comes the steel girders, the atrocities modern men call building. It is the fate of the universe. That is why it is such a pleasure to come here, to Marchmont, to dig in peace."

"With nothing to hamper you unless it be a local legend."

Codrill shot him a sly, strange look. "We have our difficulties. We are said to be desecrating sacred ground. We are said to be lunatics escaped from the local Colney Hatch. We are said to be thieves."

"It is axiomatic of your fame."

"These gaping locals have never heard of me or my discoveries."

"Their lives," Diarmid ruminated, "are still ruled by Cuimin and his men."

"Cuimin," after another speculative glance at his companion, "was a man of many parts. He came from the south."

"Some say Cornwall. Others from farther afield. Brittany, Gaul."

"In those days the boats were hardly as stout or as weatherproof as they are today."

"Men built as they needed to build. Why should they not be in advance of these so-called advanced days?"

"You prescribe to that view! I delight in finding a fellow believer. I spend hours attempting the conversion of your brother but fear I leave him untouched by my arguments."

"Padraig belongs to the species of Irish who are content to leave things as they are. They have always been; they always will be; therefore they always must. Not even the soil must be disturbed, unless it is to move Cuimin from his hallowed ground to a new site so men may cease to cross the treacherous bay in search of surcease. I confess I find myself wallowing in Irish deceptiveness. The sands of Clonmurragh are nothing to the paths Padraig and his neighbours are treading."

"You find your brother — baffling?"

"I find him far from well," replied Diarmid, "one moment writing me and describing you all as madmen, the next telling me stories of suicide and miracles and foolish blarney that no ordinary man can believe. He wants to make a pilgrimage safe in the same breath as he disowns all responsibility for the pilgrimage. Not even in Ireland does it make sense."

"I am glad you have come. It will make our task easier."

"I shall not be staying many weeks but while I am here I will do my best to unravel the tangled relationships."

"Shall we proceed? This, where we have been digging this week, is obviously the refectory. See, enough of the outer wall has been unearthed to indicate the extent. We have not yet found the fireplace but within a matter of days no doubt we shall do so."

"You're confident this was Cuimin's abbey?"

"It was an abbey," said Codrill. "Whether Cuimin's or another's must wait for the proof."

"I expected little more than proddings."

"We are keeping our findings to ourselves. You'll understand if we reveal them prematurely the plot will be inundated with sightseers, hampering our work."

"Have you told Padraig?"

"He was here yesterday."

"He tells me Father O'Rourke helps you."

"Hinders is more the appropriate word."

"Is he against Cuimin having settled here?" curious.

"He is — " Codrill stopped. Across the grass the rest of the team were streaming from the direction of the bothy.

Diarmid watched them, seeing the denims, the bleached uncovered heads, the easy fraternity of the young men and girls. One or two older men were among the party, the foreman, the overseer, men with experience, no doubt Codrill's companions in Corfu and elsewhere.

"Yes?" he encouraged.

"I was about to say in league with your brother but that sounds melodramatic. Shall I say he is constantly at Marchmont, constantly with Mr. Riall in the library, an influence in the district."

"The priest is an important member of a community, especially in Ireland."

"Not only in Ireland. I remember a padre in Corfu, a magnificently bearded priest of the Orthodox religion who indulged in the blackest of rites."

"You're not telling me Padraig indulges in magic and seances and things of that kind? I thought you were civilised,

94

Professor, pre-Roman civilisation, pure, undiluted."

A gleam of appreciation appeared in the pale blue eyes behind the rimless spectacles.

"One is safe in antique times. The necessity to step carefully and mind your tongue loses some of its double barbedness when one is dealing with primordialism."

"I doubt it," said Diarmid. "There seems enough twisting mazework to lure the bravest of men to a sticky end. But we're no longer alone." He stood to one side as the team scrambled into the dig.

"Good-morning, Charles. Good-morning, Neville. 'Morning. 'Morning." He rapidly greeted his workers. "This is Mr. Diarmid Riall, the brother of Mr. Riall. He has come for a few days to Marchmont, between designing colossal sets of temples and Egyptian pyramids. You all know of him, I'm sure."

Diarmid acknowledged the smiling greetings. "All this is very interesting. I already guessed the house was on the site of a religious order but that Cuimin actually had a community here is new. We've always worshipped on Clunare and it'll take a little time for the locals to transfer their faith."

"This doesn't alter the fact that Clunare is a holy island," added Codrill. "It merely strengthens the belief long held in archaeological circles that a man of such calibre would not remain stationary on an island the size of Clunare. When the time is ripe, I'll ask the clergy to come. The Bishop, I believe, has done much research into Cuimin's later years."

The Professor gave his orders for the day and the team moved to their stations. Soon the sound of axe and shovel disturbed the peacefulness of the valley and murmured voices broke the rhythmic echo of blade on earth. The scattered piles of earth increased and others were sifted methodically for remains of vases or utensils. A dedicated intentness filled the pasture and after a period Diarmid sat on a hump and watched the progress, endeavouring to sort all he had so far been told.

"You're very serious."

Marcia was standing beside him, notebook in hand. "It's eleven o'clock and time for cocoa. I ordered a mug for you."

"Have I earned it? I should be studying Hector's play."

"Let it be. This is more relaxing. You see how we're finding walls?"

"More than walls. A sense of existence. I've been conscious of it while I've been here, picturing Cuimin in his coarse handwoven robe, directing building operations, praying at his altar. Where exactly do you expect to find the church?"

"To the south of the refectory. It was probably joined by a frater, a kind of cloister. You must browse in the library."

He took a mug of cocoa from a denim-trousered girl.

"Thank you, Sonia," said Marcia. She sat on the grass beside his hump. "I've got five minutes. Father O'Rourke is at the house. After his session, he'll be down here."

"How do you do," said Diarmid to the dark-clothed man who had come across the pasture. "I'm Diarmid."

Father O'Rourke's voice was a country burr. " 'Tis pleased I am to meet you."

"I'm a little in the dark, Father," admitted Diarmid. "Padraig sent for me. He wrote an appealing letter about madmen sending him nearly crazy. What do I find? An organised dig, proceeding with little effect on the house, and himself full of moth-like stories. You didn't, by any chance, dictate that letter to me?"

Father O'Rourke's eyes twinkled in his round, creaseless face. "I did not expect Diarmid Riall to be an idiot."

"Thank you," said Diarmid. "You too are worried. What do you think is the matter with him?"

The black shoulders moved slightly. "Apathy. Delayed shock."

"From what?"

"Several factors. Has anyone mentioned Kirsty O'Halloran?"

"He did himself. He went with her to Dublin and lived with her for a year. Then she left him, presumably because she was carrying his child. He doesn't wish to see her or the child. What is it?"

"A boy."

"Sometime after, how long I cannot guess, Kirsty came back to Cloncobh or was brought back. Anyway, she was dying and she had herself rowed to Clunare and was cured."

"She was ill and from that moment she recovered."

"From divine interference?"

"Who are we to say?"

"Padraig said you saw her. Doctor Costain saw her. Others saw her. She had the cancer."

"That was what she said. Certainly she was wasted; there were great hollows under her eyes. She had spent several years in London."

"London," said Diarmid, "doesn't give you the cancer. Or not any more than any other place. You're not prepared to say she was actually dying?"

"My duty is to the soul."

"Exactly! Was Kirsty's soul in need of sustenance?"

"Every man's soul is in need of sustenance."

"You know what I mean."

"She was in need of a friend. The one she had served with faithfulness had died, leaving her alone."

"In London?"

"Yes, in London."

"So she ran, like a lost child, to her home and Padraig wouldn't see her?"

"She asked nothing of Padraig," sternly. "You make too much."

"I am trying to understand why I am here, Father. It is a little bewildering, all these differing accounts. I need a direction, a word to say: Go over there and dig two feet under the ground and you will find stone."

"More likely you would find nothing," said Father O'Rourke. He began to divest himself of his black coat. "I usually do an hour's digging. It is good for the soul and the muscles."

"You talk in riddles too. I suppose I must expect it. I'll away to Clunare to see if the holy island will clear my conundrums."

"St. Cuimin had no truck with self-seekers," said the Father. He took up a spade and joined a group; then he relented: "He loved a fighter, though. Perhaps that was why he interceded for Kirsty O'Halloran. She's a fighter, by the Virgin. More's the pity, Padraig will never see her. I shall go on trying betimes."

So, estimated Diarmid, as he moved across the sward, one of the reasons for Father O'Rourke's visits to Marchmont had been delved. It made him all the more eager in his turn to see Kirsty O'Halloran.

5

FIRST however he was going to Clunare. The glimpse that morning of the sacred island through the gap in the hills had dictated it. He went indoors and collected Hector's manuscript and a package of food from Mrs. Sullivan. "You want to get Donal Murphy to row you over," she told him. When he asked what was the matter with his arms, she retorted: "There's currents there, Mr. Diarmid. They trapped your mother." A weighty answer which quietened his protests. On impulse, he knocked on the library door as he passed but Padraig was not there. He paused, undecided, scanning the rows of leather-bound books. He would need more than a few days to read these wordy tomes. Marcia must instruct him as to the volumes to choose.

He had been going to ask for his mother's journal. The shrine at Clunare, he felt, was the atmosphere and the sanctuary needful to understand her agony of heart. However, he did not know where it was. Then he saw a volume on a table by a window, red-bound, with a clasp, open at a page of confession. The writing was vaguely familiar. He stepped forward and saw: '*I was told today what I have feared for some time*'. He closed it quickly, and put it in his brief-case. Padraig must have left it for him. The action seemed indicative of the way Padraig had in behaving. A bleak way of disclosure.

He went along the drive. From here there was no glimpse of the dig. He turned west at the gate and walked along the narrow road, alone, but with the ghosts of many people at his elbow. Once a dog joined him and he greeted it cheerfully, talking to it in a friendly, sympathetic manner until it left him as suddenly as it had arrived. At one o'clock he reached the beach opposite Clunare and knocked at the cottage on the foreshore.

"Donal Murphy? I'm Diarmid Riall. I'm staying at the house. Can you take me over to the island?"

The young man jerked his shoulder behind him. "We're eating. Would you come in?"

"I'll wait on the beach. I have my lunch. What are the tides?"

"You'll not drown today."

Diarmid smiled. "It looks calm and placid, but I was warned not to go by myself. I can't believe the gods are angry on a day like this."

"They resent interference."

"So do I when I'm busy." He refused the double meaning in the reply. These people believed anything. It was time the west was opened up . . . and knew some of it would be spoiled.

There was a big temptation to open the journal, within sight of the spot where she had died, within a few yards of where her body had been washed up. The only line he had seen played recitatively in his mind: *'I was told today what I have feared for some time'*, but he withstood it. The beach was too bare for that personal cry. Only in the remains of Cuimin's church or on the headland beyond might he glimpse the ache of a woman condemned.

Donal came across the shingle, a big, powerful, broad-shouldered lad in thick sweater and long sea-boots.

"You'll have half an hour there," he advised.

"No longer?" disappointed.

"Tide turns at three o'clock." He began to ease the boat from its moorings.

Diarmid rose to help him. In a few moments it was floating gently on the water. Donal was in and lifting the outboard motor to the stern. The phut of the engine firing was echoed from the neighbouring rocks and the gulls, roused, wheeled in shrieking chorus over their heads.

There was a feeling of timelessness, drifting towards the rugged foreshore, after the engine had been cut out, a hundred yards from the island, carried by the outgoing tide that within the hour would turn and carry them back. Diarmid was searching the cliff for the ruin he remembered but it was too long ago; too much else had come between.

"Up the path," said Donal as he hesitated, seeking direction, "and to your left at the gap. It's rough but not as rough as it was. The parties have trampled the heather."

"Do you bring them over?"

"Me and Pat O'Brien."

"I'll see you in a while."

He climbed quickly, eager to sample the secrets of Cuimin's hallowed spot, the events of the morning playing freely within his imagination. His eyes were alert, noting the previous presence of other feet, litter in a hollow, desecrating the holiness. Why must some people toss their papers about, heedless of the treasures of others? He had seen it magnified at the stately homes, orange peel, crusts, a day's work to clear after the invasion of the masses. The London parks too, generously offered to the people by their sovereign. They would squeal if the privileges were shut off. Clunare belonged to Padraig; he allowed them to visit it, and forbore to make it part of his living; they must repay him by this flagrant lapse of manners.

Almost at the fork, he halted, looking back at the climbing, winding path and over the sea to the mainland. The old house stood, grey and remote, between the twin heights of Pins and Reek, protected from the gales, and he was affected by the sense of timelessness that was in every breath and murmur.

Clambering up the boulder-strewn path, his feet slipped on the damp, moist earth. There was a stream nearby; he could hear its gurgle in the silence, musical, intricate. Involuntarily, he began to hum a song from his childhood, an Irish crooning song that the women sang over the cradles in the low, whitewashed cottages.

He had come out on a headland. Here the breeze had freshened, ruffling his hair, whipping his cheeks to a pink, warm glow. He drew the salt tang into his lungs and thought: Hector should be here, in this paradise, drinking deep of the *pastiche*. Or Lewis and Mora, awaiting the birth of their first child. Tonight he would write to Lewis and tell him all that had happened . . . and scrambled on. Donal had said half an hour and ten minutes had gone already.

Surely he must be near the church. He sought for the ruins, seeing nothing but rocks and coarse grass and rough brambles. As he pressed forward the land fell away into a small hollow and there, on its edge, stood a heap of stones, tumbled, hardly a wall, less of a find than the hemp and wattle of the dig.

He stood in that isolated space and a peace that was in the air and in the plants and in the ground stole over him and quietened the throb of his heart and the racing of his blood.

"Are you there, St. Cuimin?" he asked, barely raising his voice. "Are you with me, forsooth? 'Tis wonderful, this feeling of being protected."

Yes, that was it. Protected. As though another presence was in that small hollow, guarding it, caring for it.

Kirsty had known it. Suddenly he knew why Kirsty had revived when she stood in this fair place, why the fears and the stresses of her life had slipped away, the cancer or whatever it had been had been erased. Nothing evil could exist in this sacred vale.

Nothing evil? He took the clasped journal and opened it. 'It is the creeping paralysis that has attacked me. Doctor Kenwood made that plain this morning. In a very short time I shall be a cripple, condemned to spend my life in a wheelchair, with Ruaidhri's gaze forever hurt and censorious. He is strong; he will never comprehend; I shall be deserted and alone'.

Had she not had children, light-hearted and gay, seeing nothing malformed in illness as they saw nothing extraordinary in good health? He would have pushed her gladly in her wheelchair, read to her, related to her his doings.

'I am not brave enough to face this alone. I must send for Colum'. And a few days later: 'Colum is coming. He is coming at once, like the dear, good man that he is. God forbid that I should be judged by my feeling for him, but it is there, outvying my love for Ruaidhri. It has stolen on me, these last few years, with every visit he has made, with the friendship that makes no demands and claims one the more. I should have met Colum before I met Ruaidhri. Then I would not be chained to this grey stone house, this queer, damp, foreign land. I made a mistake when I married Ruaidhri. He loved me, heaven confirm my agreement. He saw in me a flower to be snatched, like a boy in a country lane, and having snatched he gave it no water. I have been starved and cut off, except when Colum came. Colum has been my water, sustaining me until he came again. He is so patient and so gentle, so unlike Ruaidhri that it must be against God's will to give him my love, but I cannot help myself. When Colum is here, I am alive; I can do anything; my will and my strength take fresh courage'.

A pathetic entry: 'This evening I fell down in the hall. My legs gave way beneath me. Ruaidhri was harsh and disciplinary, having no sympathy, yet I saw him watching me fearfully as I forced them to carry me from the dining-room to the drawing-room. "Will you play tonight, Elinore?" he asked. I had to tell him, before Colum has come, before my strength is exhausted. It was as I feared. He had no understanding. "A cripple in a wheelchair, Elinore? What nonsense is this? We will have Doctor Kenwood." I informed him I have had Doctor Kenwood. "Then a specialist from Dublin."

'He was like a mad thing. He instructed Doctor Kenwood to summon a specialist. "If that fails," he tossed out, "we'll take her to Dublin." It was his way of attesting me with the folly that had pursued me. In times of bleakness these Rialls are bewitched; they seek surcease from the ancient remedies of their ancestors. There is nothing I would not do but with Colum's gentle accompaniment, not Ruaidhri's strident shouting. The look in his eyes is a further accusation. I have failed him; I am to become a helpless cripple, when he needed more sons to wrest from this peaty soil a grandeur that is slipping with each year that goes by. Could we not go to Dublin, I enquire, shut up the Royal and take a residence so that with treatment maybe I should be less useless? A year in Dublin would recompense me for my sentence . . . and Colum is in Dublin."

The entry was pitiful. In her extremity, she turned to Colum, urbane, city-bred. He it was who took her to Dublin, to the specialist who confirmed the diagnosis and gave her a period of twelve months before her legs failed her completely. Thereafter she knew her arms and the rest of her body would follow until she lay, a living death in the midst of virility and strength.

Poor, sweet, lost, little mother. Diarmid could not blame her for taking her pleasure while she could, nor have too much censure for Cousin Colum who loved her as deeply as her husband ever had. On Clunare the unrelenting triangle was simple, inevitable; the one man too strong, the other too weak, while between them, caught in the grip of the incurable disease, the fragrant English flower.

He turned the pages, skimming the weeks in Dublin, the return to Marchmont, the gradual enfeebling of the failing spirit, the horror and disgust of Ruaidhri as he saw his hopes crumbling to dust. Through the carefully written account came the agony and incredulity of the fit, prompting the fiery outbursts. "Cannot you be more careful, Elinore!" Passionate, frustrated, pathetic, the cry of a man at grips with an illness he could not envisage. Strong men feared illness more than death, and his father had been robust, carousing with the neighbours. Yet as well he had been a cultured man; his intellect should have told him what his fated Irish whimsy refused to face. In other words, his world was awry and he did what other men in similar circumstances would do; he buried his lips in his whisky glass and refused to admit it.

So to the last week. A shaft of sunshine

was resting on all that remained of Cuimin's altar. Diarmid lifted his head and saw it and took comfort from the sign.

'Colum has come. He is aghast at the rapidity of the disease and anxious regarding the future. With him here, I am more resigned. Could he not stay, give up his practice in Dublin and take one in Dunphilly? I am demented with my longing to keep him with me. I am frail and in fear, not of the helplessness, but of his departure. That is wrong. I should be having Ruaidhri's support, not calling out for his cousin to come. But he comes; every time I write, he comes, like the faithful soul that he is. May God forgive me and lend me strength in this last trial'.

'We sat in the garden and tried to talk of the future. There are the boys; they must have their careers. Colum has promised, if and when I am no longer here, to intercede for them with Ruaidhri. "You must not fear," he assured me. "Ruaidhri loves them, as he loves you. This has been tragic for him too. He had that streak in him that must hide from blunt truth; he is beside himself with worry and dementia."

'*That streak in him that must hide from*

blunt truth'. How true and how descriptive was that of Padraig, pulling the wool across his eyes, viewing the universe with secrets in his heart; in his case, the truth of Kirsty and the child; in Ruaidhri's, the incurable disease of their mother.

A fraction of the curtain slipped away from Diarmid and he began to see a way in which to lift the strain. However, time was passing. He glanced at his watch. Twenty minutes since he had left Donal but many years in the living, the gaining of knowledge.

'As we sat there Ruaidhri came and we talked together, Ruaidhri and Colum especially, in sober tones, arranging what should happen to Padraig and Diarmid if the severing should come rather quicker than later. I was possessed of a great calm. They could be friends; the hot fire in Ruaidhri had quite gone this evening and he was his lively, friendly, welcoming self that I have known in the great happiness of our marriage. The house too was relaxed, basking in the late summer sunshine. It approved, I thought, the two Rialls. Ruaidhri gave me his arm and I mounted the stairs without too much strain. In the bedroom he took me in his arms and lifted me into bed. "I have been ill of the temper," he confessed, "because of my fears, but we will find a way. There is still Cuimin," he teased. "Shall we give you to Cuimin to mend or to break . . . ?"

'He has gone back to the library, to spend an hour with his books. Colum is below on the terrace, smoking a last cigar. I can smell the aroma through my open window. Why can I not die now, when my men are at peace, when there is no ill-will between them? Another week and the devil will have entered the rooms. Nothing that Cuimin or any other saint can do will ease the thunder and the storm that will rage when this mood of Ruaidhri's has subsided. We must go to Clunare and if I do not come back . . . It is an idea, a slip on the path up which Colum must carry me, a false move in the boat when his arm is not round me . . . Would that be cowardice? Should I think thus? My crippling is bad. I upset a glass of claret this evening. Ruaidhri was forbearing but I saw him shrink. A small token but significant. Nay, I must not think thus. Padraig and Diarmid are young and when one is young one is resilient. One can accept departure . . .'

Lastly: 'A glorious morning. I can see Clunare through the gap, clear as an agate, beckoning me to its fastness. I will go with Colum and we will take what comes'.

From below came an echoing shout. He called back, jerked from the past.

"I do not believe," softly, "that you chose the sea, Mother, deliberately, together. There is too much hope here, on Cuimin's island, to choose to slip or step aside. Something occurred, the wind came up, the tide turned, you tried to move, Colum rose to help you and the boat upturned . . ."

He was no nearer a true explanation of the tragedy. The official verdict had been accidental death, as published in the *Dunphilly Times*. Aunt Ma-Ma had had a copy; he had read it, frowning over the stilted wording. "Would you consider — ?" A question to a witness. His father, bereaved, in the box, spitting out his replies. "Colum Riall was my cousin. He was often at the house." The sliced pride. *'There is a streak that must hide from blunt truth'.*

He went swiftly down the path to where Donal waited.

"The tide has turned."

"I'm coming." He settled into the prow. "Was the boat that was used when my mother died similiar to this?"

Donal showed no surprise at the question. "One of O'Brien's, without an engine."

"And a storm came up?"

"They should never have gone," said Donal. "The wind was off-shore. 'Tis dangerous these waters are then. You mind the time when Lifty Callaghan defied his father and was carried to the rocks below the Luce?"

"I mind the time when I defied my father and my mother cried all night. How then did they reach Clunare? Or did they never do so?"

"There's no telling," said Donal. "Nobody saw them go. It came up, sudden, out of the west, and in a twinkling they were gone."

"If no one saw them . . ." began Diarmid.

"It's the telling I'm relating," obtusely.

"Men's tongues err. My mother says

it was a beautiful morning. Like today. The island could be seen from the house. There's no danger today."

"I'm just telling — " said Donal.

"It is odd," remarked Diarmid, "it should be so calm when they set out and in so short a time they were upturned — "

"Unless . . ." said Donal.

"There is suspicion then. I don't believe it. She had an incurable disease. Did you know that?"

"I did not, Mr. Diarmid. Like Kirsty O'Halloran?"

"What do you know of Kirsty?"

"That she came to Clunare and was cured."

"Did you carry her?"

"Me and Pat O'Brien. We carried her afloat and we put her on Clunare and she went up to the shrine."

"Alone?" he asked.

"With the power of Cuimin beside her."

"I must see Kirsty. There was no storm when you returned?"

"The sea was like a pond. Kirsty sat with her eyes a-shine and her tongue saying: 'I have seen a great light, Donal, and I am well.' So she was, Mr. Diarmid. She walked up the shore."

"She walked up Clunare."

"You would doubt me, for sure?"

"I'm not doubting you. Your story is corroborated. Other people saw Kirsty. Nobody saw my mother."

"That was a tragedy, Mr. Diarmid."

"For my father, indeed. He shut himself away, they say, and had no more enjoyment. He sent my brother and I to relations. It was a pity because my mother had no intention of hurting him. She was sadly ill and would have died. By drowning she was spared years of painful suffering while he was spared the agony of seeing her die. The end was swift. Knowing what I do now I can be grateful to God. But there was Colum and he and my father were cousins. They both loved my mother. I am afraid, Donal, we shall never know what happened on Clunare or in the bay that long ago day."

"Mr. Colum Riall was a strong swimmer," said Donal. He was staring ahead at the mainland coast.

"Under tempestuous conditions? I think we must assume she pulled him down.

She would be a dead weight with her paralysed limbs. Battered and tossed, he would stand little chance of survival. Let them rest. Does Padraig come here at all?"

"I haven't seen him for weeks, Mr. Diarmid. Since the dig," with a chuckle, "he's been occupied at the Royal."

"You know his idea? That an abbey at Marchmont will isolate Clunare and free it from its curious visitors. Superintendent Mulligan has said the crossing is too suicidal and has taken too many lives."

"If people would only listen to wisdom," began Donal. The boat touched the beach and he jumped out, hauling it up the shingle.

"When that happens, the world will be safe for lunatics," smiled Diarmid. "Thank you, Donal. I shall want you again. I haven't finished with Clunare. It seems an ideal spot to work in, if Cuimin gives me his approval."

"He was a gentle saint."

"With an armour of spears. No man in those days could exist without faith and without fear. An avenging saint, methinks, who did not put out a hand to save his followers. Maybe they laughed, at his shrine, delighting in their freedom. I have a feeling that he was like all men, Donal, beset by nagging notions, kind to some and cruel to others. Erase his legend and he would not be vastly different from us now."

He went back towards Marchmont but when he had reached the gate he did not turn in but continued on towards Cloncobh, coming in a quarter of an hour to the church and the graveyard. An old crone was bending over a grave. He bade her good-day and made his way to a distant corner where rows of leaning stones told of Rialls dead and buried. The most recent was still clean and erect. Connemara marble, he saw, erected by Padraig. '*To the memory of Ruaidhri Riall of Marchmont Royal who departed this life . . .*' He moved to the other side. '*To the everlasting memory . . .*' but it was blank. No record there of the English flower. He searched rapidly, energetically, pulling aside briars and docks that had clogged the graves. Dermot Riall. Peader Riall. Clodagh Riall. Patrick Riall. An earlier Diarmid, died 1676. A lot of Padraigs. Several Cormacs and Hughs; but of Elinore, of Colum . . . In a corner, almost neglected, the simple wooden cross leaned brokenly, the lettering faded, well-nigh undecipherable: *'Colum Riall, drowned in Clunare Bay . . .'* He turned the cross. Nothing else. He searched again. Then he approached the crone.

"I'm Diarmid Riall. I'm looking for my mother's grave."

Her skin was dried and withered by the fire on her hearth, the colour of mahogany, dark, stained, ingrained. Her gums were toothless, her eyes dim and watery.

" 'Tis so," she mumbled and pawed him with long-clawed hands. "The little Diarmid, grown so tall, grown into a man."

"Should I know you?" hastily seeking his remembrance. Biddy? Patsy? Who else had there been at the Royal? Siobahn Foley, his mother's maid? This, Siobahn? No, it could not be. But, yes. She was babbling on: "A sweet, dear child, the spit of her dear soul, laughing and merry the whole day long. Sure and it's grateful I am to be seeing you with these poor eyes that see nothing much; 'tis thankful I am to be feeling you with these fingers that have the rheumatics; 'tis joyful I am to be hearing your voice, the bells that rang in hers and never rang when she was laid to rest."

"Is she buried here? My father's stone, and Colum's cross, but nothing of her ..."

" 'Tis not here," she replied. " 'Twas never here."

"Not here?" He paused. "You mean, they never found her? She's buried in the bay, with the water for her grave, the skies for her witness?"

"Nay, alanna," she croaked. "The sea gave her up and she was calm; she lay smiling in her sleep and the weakness was gone; they took her to Marchmont and the master would not have her. The sorrow of it! The sadness of it! Refused her the entrance to his house, the cruel, sour beastie that he was. 'She went from me,' he cried out. 'Take her where she went. I'll not have her again. I'll not have her near me.' He was in torment, the poor, wee, distraught man. Never a sight would he have of the Father, and there she lay, on his threshold, and he shut the door and drank himself asleep."

Diarmid's hurt was throbbing in his throat. A fine Christian way to treat his mother, indeed.

"His brother was here," went on Siobahn, her poor rheumy eyes peering at him from their quivering lids. "He said: 'For sure, she must be buried, Ruaidhri. Why not take her to Clunare? She has been there, with Colum. Let Cuimin be having her, in the fastnesses of the island'."

"It's holy land."

"Och!" she agreed. "The Bishop would never be having it. Father McWhelan — him that was here before Father O'Rourke — would have none of it either. So Patrick, the saints preserve and guard him, took her and laid her to rest near the shrine of St. Cuimin and there she lies, in the peace of his wing, the dear, good, sweet soul."

With nothing for her epitaph but the green grass and the grey rocks and the wild flowers and the gulls sweeping overhead and the old stones that had once carried the vessels of communion and known Cuimin's rough hands. A grave untouched, unfouled, unconsecrated, and yet con-secrated by the word of God, long years ago, hallowed ground, in which to lie content. Her lips had smiled; she had died content. Dear Lord! He breathed shakily, touched almost beyond words: "Thank you, Siobahn. Thank you, Uncle Patrick."

Unevenly, he asked: "Then why should Colum, if not my mother — ?"

The cracked laugh split like a dozen fragments. "He came up, weeks later, with his teeth set and his body writhing in his struggles, and the Bishop said he had died a Christian and gave his blessing, but Ruaidhri, God plague his hard soul, would have no stone. A wooden cross and nothing more. His brother had the words painted on, him who sailed a great ship. He came and was at the big house and 'twas said he told Ruaidhri a bushel of truths but never a sight did we have of Ruaidhri, either here or at Marchmont. He had parted the two and that was the end."

And so Column lay here, amongst the Rialls, acknowledged and respected, and Elinore lay at Clunare, unacknowledged but at peace. Walking back to the Royal, Diarmid had the feeling that in the shadow of St. Cuimin, his mother was the gainer. He would not disturb her but would find her grave and kneel beside it and join with the early saint in thanking God for the beautiful wonders of the universe and in his heart he would know that of all the places in Ireland where his mother would have chosen to lie, if she could not return to her native England, she would have chosen Clunare, under the blue skies and within reach of the unattainable.

6

HE had taken the local bus from Cloncobh and jolted along the high-banked roads beneath the fuchsia hedges in company with women and baskets and squawking hens and dogs. At Nuamaris the market claimed him until he caught another bus to Dunphilly. Father O'Rourke, come to inspect the previous day's digging, had given him the address.

"She may not see you," he warned.

"I shall have to risk that," replied Diarmid.

"When she knows you're a Riall, she may shut the door."

"If she does, I shall be surprised. She will not be the Kirsty O'Halloran I have been hearing about."

The house was in the long, bleak street. Why, he asked involuntarily, were Irish streets so bleak, so devoid of character, so shorn of attraction? The grey slate roofs, the plain drab rows — he might have been in any small town. His footsteps rang on the pavement, dying away as he halted to look at the numbers. Kirsty's was twenty-seven. He was on the even side. Across the street he saw a different house, a building of less plain proportions, Georgian. How did it come to be there, like a jewel in the surrounding dust?

Without a doubt, it must be Kirsty's. How he knew he did not pause to question. He rang the bell and waited for the front door to be opened. When it was, a skinny little maid peeped out at him.

"Good-morning," he said. He raised his hat which he had donned for his visit. "Is Miss O'Halloran in?"

"Nobody lives here of that name, sir."

"Oh." He met her eye speculatively. "Then — can I meet your mistress? She was Miss O'Halloran once, of Cloncobh. I've come from there." Should he give her his card? Or would that destroy the chance of seeing Kirsty? "I'm not peddling washing machines or hawking vacuum cleaners," he countered. He offered the card. "She'll know the name," and prayed to St. Cuimin she would also see him. "Will you go and tell her? I've made a special journey. I'm only in this part for a few days."

The little thing vanished and he stood on the step and watched a man with a donkey farther along the street. Otherwise, the road was deserted. Nobody in this part of the world appeared to be busy, unless they had gone to Nuamaris to the market.

"She's sorry, sir. She's not seeing anybody — " The maid was back, returning him his card.

He said deliberately: "Tell her it's her brother-in-law, on an urgent matter." This time he knew she would see him.

"Will you come this way, sir?"

He stepped into the hall. It was pure Regency. Kirsty O'Halloran, or whatever she was called, lived in some state. "You'll love her," said Marcia. He followed the little maid into a room filled with sunshine and gasped as its quintessence was revealed.

By the window a woman was standing, a well-built, sturdy, well-to-do woman, attired in prosperous clothes, not at all the kind of person he had expected to see. In a voice from which all trace of accent had vanished, she enquired: "What can

I do for you? I have no decorating to be done."

Touché, he thought. Reacting to the slight, he said: "I'm sorry to intrude — "

"If you wish to speak of Padraig, I am impervious to his whims."

"He doesn't know I'm here."

She looked at him with eyes in which the sum of experience was full. This woman, he saw, had suffered and suffered much. He was ashamed of having so much as dared to enter her house without invitation.

"I'd better go." He turned on his heel.

"No," plainly. "Now you're here, you'll have some refreshment. The journey from Cloncobh is a jolting one. You came by bus?"

"Padraig had the car," he replied.

"Will you sit down?"

"Thank you." He cast his eyes appreciatively about the room. This was futile. He would have done better to keep away. She was nothing to the Rialls . . . and heard again Padraig's strangled voice. "Kirsty is real!" Yes, she was real, a woman who had been beyond the veil and returned, to face the man she had lived with, and had joy flung remorselessly in her face.

"A little Irish whisky?" Her mouth curved in the beginning of a smile. "You would not be a true Riall if you refused. You'll be the son who was sent to England. I've read about you. Creating wonderments for the society."

"I should be designing a set now, for Conal O'Bridie's new play, *The Irish Room.*"

"Haven't you inspiration at Marchmont?"

"Kirsty!" He leaned forward. "Must we hedge? Padraig told me his side. I'll not hope for yours."

"You can have it," she told him. "It's no longer of any consequence. I was a stupid girl, thinking I could carry off what older and better women have failed to do. Who was I, an O'Halloran, to go with a Riall of Marchmont Royal?"

"You could have given him — all."

"Instead of which he gave me hell."

"Did you really leave him because of — because of — " he hesitated.

"I left him," she said, "because I should never have gone at all. His place was at Marchmont."

"Our father refused him."

"There were ways."

"You did not think thus when he came knocking at your door."

"In the pouring rain, desperate and deceived. I tell you it's over. I never want to think of it again. He was a poor thing, not worth the trouble of our talking about him."

"He's my brother." He stared at her closely. "Our mother loved him. You loved him."

"I did not."

He went on forcibly: "You did, Kirsty. Why else would you go with him, defy Father McWhelan, your parents, live with him in a back street in the city, lie with him — "

"Stop!" she cried. She whipped at him, violently: "I tell you I'm finished. I've gone a long way since then."

"So has he. The tragedy began when our mother was ill. You know, I presume, she had an incurable illness."

"Did she now?" The anger receded from her lips. "The poor, wee, lonely woman, with that man for a husband."

"It's nothing very complicated," said Diarmid. He told her of the journal and the trip to Clunare. "She's buried on Cuimin's isle. I would not wish her elsewhere."

"Nor myself," breathed Kirsty.

"There were she and Father and Cousin Colum, and this dreadful disease crippling her so that she knew she was doomed."

"She would not choose death."

"You think like I do — ?"

"Listen, Diarmid. After years with Alice Shane and her brother I was told I had the cancer. I was his housekeeper but he educated my son and there was nothing he did not discuss with me. He was an artist. You may have heard of him. Amos Brierley."

"Amos Brierley!" he cried. "You were with him! I've been to his house in Hampstead. You've heard of Adam Greuzer?"

"He was a particular friend of Amos'."

"His partner is Lewis Hope. Lewis and I were at Cambridge together. Their galleries are the finest in London."

"Amos' pictures hung in Greuzer's gallery. He wanted to paint me but I never would wish it."

"Oh, Kirsty, you should. What a stir you would have caused in the Royal Academy."

"He used my body," said Kirsty, "and paid me. Lash me now, Diarmid Riall."

But he was smiling gently. "I'm not shocked," he replied. "I know of dozens who would willingly sit for Amos Brierley and take not a penny. Why is there any shame in letting a master use the gifts God has given you? To some a percipient brain, an art with fingers; to others a beauty of form. Tell me," he was thinking back, remembering a certain furore, "Aphrodite?"

"You know too much, Diarmid Riall."

"I know nothing. I am here to be informed. To think you were with Amos Brierley, cooking his meals. Those delicious macaroons! Were they your doing?"

"Even in the days at Cloncobh I was a good cook."

"Padraig should have kept you. What a mistress you'd have made for the Royal."

"I had finished with that. When I took him to Dublin, I shed that skin. What rubbish you are talking! You are like all the Rialls, dreaming and fanciful. An O'Halloran at Marchmont!"

"Times have changed. You became Amos' housekeeper."

"Because I had served his sister. You little know my apprenticeship."

He sipped the whisky and waited.

"I wish often I had stayed with Padraig. His many-sidedness would have been nothing to the singleness of Alice Shane's protection. She was a woman with a self-confessed mission; her whole life was given to saving the fallen."

"You weren't fallen."

"I had forsaken home and family and gone with a man above my station. God forgive me," she said. "He idolised his mother. You knew that?"

"Not until this week, not until he told me of her illness."

"He is afraid of pain. He lives in fear and trembling lest some such evil will touch him. He is prey to false imaginings."

"You're not immune then — ?"

"Even then," continued Kirsty, "he was the same. That household at Glenmoy was no home for him. They should not have parted you."

"Aunt Ma-Ma would have stood no nonsense."

"Padraig needed a firmness. If I stood out, he would follow, though time after time we had great quarrels. It was a squallsome time, we had, and him no more in love with me than with that Brigid Malone."

"He said you were cruel," said Diarmid. "He said you said: 'You're like the rest of that landowning bunch'."

"I was trying to rouse him, put life into him. I knew no other way."

"You were not so ignorant," he mused, "that you did not know how to get him."

"He needed no getting. He came and gave himself, flung himself at me. I had to go, to get him out of my home, to protect him from my parents. My father would have harmed him and brought scandal on us all. But when the child was coming, I knew I was wrong. I had thought myself clever . . . and God proved me false. I had my employment, with Mrs. Shane. Mrs. O'Halloran, I was to her; it was better so. She saw the birth as an end of my service. 'Kirsty', she said, 'you have been a good servant. If there is any way in which I can help you at any time . . .' I thanked her and said, Could I stay until the seventh month? Once she asked if she could visit my home and meet my husband but I told her he was away from the city; it would be better to wait until he was back. The lies I told, Diarmid, and the state I got myself into. I wanted the child, but I did not want it for him. I would be without employment and he would never get to the university.

"More and more I was seeing it would never do; I was not the woman for him; I must cut the knot and leave him so he was free. He was unhappy in his employment; he flung into furious tempers; he accused me of mis-shaping his life. How then could a child, born in such circumstances, add to the comfort? I must go. But how? I paced the streets; I considered ending my life in the Liffey but that would cause notoriety, publicity to Padraig and further calumny for his father. I must slip away in the night, pray he would realise ..." She laughed harshly. "Who ever heard of a Riall having sense? But that was in the future. An opportunity was offered me suddenly. Mrs. Shane asked me one day if I could accompany her to London. Her brother, an artist, was holding an exhibition of paintings and had asked her to go. Onny her personal maid was ill with the shingles; Sarah Ryan who might have gone had her

mother and young sister; could I go?
Would my husband mind? My husband,
I said, would be pleased at the chance.
Would I be away long? A week, two
weeks, a month? That would bring me
to the seventh month. If my child could
be born in England, would it not help to
solve my problems?

— "So I wrote a letter to Padraig, saying
it would be criminal not to go, that when
I had finished with Mrs. Shane I would
find other employment. I hoped he would
understand but I was Kirsty O'Halloran
and he was Padraig Riall and the two could
never mix. I would see that the child was
well cared for and if in the future he wanted
it with him he was to write. I imagined
it was a fine, clever letter but I have seen
since it was cruel. I took away at one stroke
the only security he had had since he left
Ruaidhri Riall."

Her voice was low but completely
audible. Going on, she said: "I went to
London with Mrs. Shane and what did she
do, the first day we were there, but break
her hip by falling from a taxi in St. James'
and spend her visit in a private nursing
home in Highgate. It was retribution for

what I had done. Thinking to escape, I was in a worse state than I had been with Padraig, unable to accept employment because of my condition, Mrs. Shane unfit to see me for the first five days, but by then," her lips curved upward with a slender omniscience at their corners, "I had been engaged as a housekeeper to Amos Brierley. It doesn't take long to tell," she confessed. "I was in the hall when he came back from the nursing home, distracted, as well he might be, for he was fond of his sister and he had all the anxiety of the exhibition on his mind. Could I get him anything? I asked. A strong whisky and soda; he would take it in the study. That was all that evening. He retired to his room. In the morning, I went down to the kitchen to find myself refreshment. Within a few hours I should know my fate.

"The kitchen was hot; the cook was sarcastic; I was not feeling well after the excitement and flurry of the accident. In the garden, I tried to assure myself that Mrs. Shane, when she had recovered, would realise my predicament. I never knew what possessed me to wander in the direction of the studio. My training must have told me it was private property, none of my business, that it should have been locked to my inquisitive fingers. I ask myself sometimes what prompted me to go into that high, light room, to walk amongst those fine canvases, to touch those brushes and rags. When a woman is nearing her time she is fey and given to strange delusions. The studio, that morning, seemed a harbour and a refuge, a world apart from the angry ocean of Padraig and the storm-tossed waves of my spirit; the portraits and paintings, rejected by Amos for his exhibition, were as magic to my wondering eyes. I had strayed into some fairyland. I was loth to leave it. Further madness possessed me. I lay on a couch and imagined myself mistress of this domain, though not in those words."

"You had beauty," said Diarmid. "They told me in the village — "

"I must have slept, weary with my worryings. Anyway, suddenly, I was awake and sat up, to find Amos had been sketching me. The shame of myself! My cheeks raged; the hotness flowed over me. 'What must I do to keep you?' he asked, and I would have fled, save he put out a hand and stayed me. His wrist was like steel. 'Nay,' he remarked, 'I do not want to buy you, unless I must.' I was apologising for my behaviour, my words tumbling pell-mell from my lips. He merely laughed at me. He was a man of thirty-five, tolerant and successful. His firm, facile hands were on my shoulders, turning me to meet his admiring eyes. 'Sir,' I cried, 'I am carrying another man's child!' 'Ye gods, so you are! Does Alice know?' I was caught; there was nothing but a clean breast of it. 'She'll ship me back,' I said. 'And you don't want to go back?' he asked. 'I can't go,' I implored. 'I've torn my ticket.' He sat down on the sofa. 'Come here, Kirsty,' he said. 'How much use would you be here?' I gasped. 'Here, in your house, with you?' He nodded. 'We'll give you a title. Housekeeper, shall it be? My house-keeper, Kirsty O'Halloran.' He chuckled, highly amused, but then as swiftly he was sober. 'There'll be nothing wrong, Kirsty. You're a lovely person,' he mused, 'lovely to look at. Can I paint you?' I was in a positive sweat of dishonour. 'Not so that anyone would recognise me. I'd die of shame.' He was preposterous but kind, understanding but hasty. 'Your body and another's head? How's that, Kirsty? The respectable housekeeper and the unacknowledged model? What a secret! Only you and I will know. Now, tell me about this Padraig. I feel sorry for him. 'You need not waste your time on him,' I snapped. 'He's no loss.' Forgive me, Diarmid. The relief was so shattering, I'd have done anything for him."

"I hope he repaid your faith," dryly, shaking his head. "Amos Brierley? Those famous pictures then, Minerva and Sybil, were you?"

She said quietly: "Worth a thousand pounds each at the present time."

She had cause for irony; and Padraig good cause for pity. The perversity of the situation!

"Amos always said I was his talisman. After I became his housekeeper" — as though taunting him — "his star mounted the heavens; he could do nothing ill. His studio was always full; his purchasers there before their paintings were dry. 'Kirsty, my love,' he would say. Yes, he loved me; he loved me as a man is meant to love a woman, with wonder, idolatrously.

If I were there, he performed his best work. He could do a painting in a day, if I were there, and earn five hundred pounds for it. No wonder he would not let me go."

"Did you want to go?"

"Often," she confessed. "It was too good, Diarmid. It was as though the sun never set, the sky never clouded. You know the feeling? Somewhere, at some moment, God would take His revenge. Time after time I said I must go; he would not let me; I would disrupt his career. Why must I go when both of us were happy? Alice Shane had gone back to Ireland. We had told her we were writing to Padraig. She had no reason to doubt us. There was no way of his discovering; in my official capacity I was Kirsty O'Halloran; when she paid another visit we could think of another explanation for Padraig's absence. I was wicked, I know, but I had found a home for myself and for Sean; I had found a person who did not condemn me for a fool or if he did he did not forever taunt me with it. He saw in me some vision he had been seeking and I should have been inhuman to destroy it. I could scarcely believe my good fortune, especially when

Sean was born, and he became a permanent member of the household."

" 'Motherhood' ?" said Diarmid.

"You know it? It was painted when he was six months old. From the first he was a good baby, never disturbing Amos when he was working. But the war came. Into our happy household dropped the ultimatum of doom. He was asked to be an official war-artist. 'I must go, Kirsty,' he said. 'Keep my house for me.' Alanna, I was lonely when he had gone. I never realised until then how much I depended on his kindness. It was like Hades, those empty rooms, that empty studio. I thought to go then, Diarmid. I could not bear the loneliness and there was the bombing and Sean. Could I not get employment in Ireland, away from the war? Something with the Red Cross? Actually, I was on the point of going when he walked in. 'Where to, Kirsty?' he said, looking down at me. 'Going away? Deserting the ship?' He put such scorn in those eyes of his that I shrivelled inside. 'I'm only to packing disused things,' I replied. ' 'Tis foolish to have so many lying about.' The bad tongue of me! I had so many possessions I could count them on two hands. 'Oh,' he said. 'I thought you were leaving. For a moment, I was afraid.' Then he went off to the war in Africa, to paint pictures with sand, he described."

"I've seen them," said Diarmid. "In the Imperial War Museum, wide, burning, flaring canvases. Everybody says he was the finest artist of the war."

"He wasn't keen to go," said Kirsty. "I could see that. 'London's the place for me,' he said, and under his breath: 'With Kirsty O'Halloran.' God forgive me, Diarmid, I lay with him the night. He begged me to. 'I may not come back, Kirsty. I may stop a bullet. Be kind to me, Kirsty,' caressing me with his tongue. It was a cruel, sweet, loving, delicious tongue, like the waters in Clunare Bay, sucking me under. 'Do you love me, Kirsty?' he said. 'Say you love me. I'll not hurt you,' he said, 'not a hair on your head. You're too precious. I'll paint you tomorrow, not your body only, but the whole of you. Lovely, desirable Kirsty.' 'Tis wicked we were, Diarmid, taking what was not ours; blinded to the awareness of God."

"Men will forgive you," murmured Diarmid.

"There's the painting," she said, and he saw the portrait on the wall, behind the window, half hidden from the light.

"Kirsty!" he cried, "it's wasted there. It wants to be in the sunshine, over here where it can be seen. It's beautiful." Awed, he gazed on the created beauty of the girl. "You'll love her," said Marcia. Amos had loved her. "I know the rest," he offered. "He never came back from the desert. He was killed flying to a forward position. It was in the papers. And his paintings became valuable."

"We were punished," said Kirsty. "The Lord abides but He is just. The telegram arrived one evening in November when the trees were bare and a nasty fog hung over London. I had taken Sean for a walk and we came in shivering with the cold, and the house was damp, not as he had ever liked it. 'Come back,' I said. 'Come back and warm it. It's too much for a woman and a child.' It was a big, tall house, too big for him, but he liked it; he wanted a big house to put his pictures in, to tell him he was a success. Diarmid, he was vain, strutting his stage, and the Lord took away his dear vanity."

"You're too hard, Kirsty," he said. "He wasn't the only one killed. In wartime we must expect to lose . . ."

"Not him, Diarmid, with the magic in his fingers and the special smile in his eyes for me, his 'Kirsty-smile', he called it and I knew when it was there he was pleased. The telegram came and I stood with it in my hands and the world went black because it could only mean one thing. He had gone. I was alone again. I must go, with my child. Diarmid, the pit of despair! You've never been in it? Black as night and clammy as death. I wanted to die. Instead of which, I sent for Mrs. Shane and lived the next few weeks in a numbness, a cringing shame."

"Why shame, Kirsty? You had cared for him royally. There was no shame."

"It was God's punishment for the ease and the contentment. And, as if that were not enough, he left me a thousand pounds. 'To my housekeeper, Kirsty O'Halloran, for her forethought and kindness during her service in my house.' The dear, good man! I wanted to hide my face and run

away and forget it all. I can never forget
Alice Shane's surprise. 'My brother has
left you a thousand pounds, Kirsty.' In
that low, stinging tone that cut you to the
heart. Her disbelieving eyes bored into
me. Dear Lord, I thought, she'd see it all,
the lovingness, the companionship, the
hours in the studio. 'I scarcely think — '
she said but I cut in, proud: 'I've served
him well, Mrs. Shane.' She looked at me
then and I felt naked. Often I had stood
before Amos and he had painted me and
my body had seemed a natural thing but in
Alice Shane's view I was contaminated. 'I
will arrange for you to have the money
shortly, Kirsty, and then you can leave.'
She was like a judgment. 'I should have
thought, with a husband — ' and I saw
her allusion. 'There's been nothing like
that, Mrs. Shane. Do you think I'd remain
here if there had been? Your brother was
a gentleman.' God forgive me, my voice
cracked. 'My husband has not been near
me for years and if you must know he was
only a boy from my village who wanted
mothering.' The canker was in me. I
never stopped to consider my words.
'Give me the money,' I said, 'and I'll

be away, me and the boy, to plague you never again.' She looked at me queerly but she held her tongue; she was plainly aghast at my lashing; but it was ill-contrived. In his house, where there had been nothing of spite; if we had disagreed, we had remained friendly. 'I must not upset you, Kirsty,' he would say. ' 'Tis more than my life's worth'."

"So you went?" murmured Diarmid.

"I did not. It was she who departed. We had a raid that night and she was terrified, hiding under the bed. 'Tis true the house shook but what of it; it shook every night, setting back on its haunches with the dawn. 'I'll leave you in charge, Kirsty,' she said. 'Mr. Malden will have instructions as to the disposal of the property.' He was the solicitor, a friend of Amos. He did not like her either. We watched her go, in a taxi she had sent for, and Sean put out his tongue at her and I wanted to, the hard, gloating, crass-hearted woman that she was. Begrudging me a thousand pounds of the fortune Amos had made through painting my body. The air was cleaner and though it was a sadness and a penance to go through his belongings and see them go, some to the museums, some to the salerooms, I would not have avoided the duty. It was as though he was there, superintending the crating. 'Not that one, Kirsty. That's for Manchester. I promised Sir Edgar.' The wishing chair was for Dublin. 'I went to Bushmills once,' he said, 'and wished I might have a true love. Are you my true love?' The wicked teasing of him. 'I am the mother of Sean,' I would say, 'and your housekeeper.' Then his lips would curl. 'Miss Kirsty O'Halloran. Or do we prefer Mrs. O'Halloran, as in the trade? The world shall acknowledge you one day, Kirsty. There'll come a day when even I will lose my patience.' The dear, kind, sweet soul of him! He never had a chance to lose his patience. I admired him for it. Him the great painter and me, the Irish girl. Don't laugh, I beg you. 'Twas no laughing matter, him falling for the girl who had gone away with Padraig Riall, and conducting himself as a gentleman should, biding his time till his friends and his acquaintances would have me. It came to me in the night, after he was gone, that he meant to do it, that there was a moment beyond which he would demand . . ."

"You'd have done it, Kirsty ?"

She lowered her head. " 'Tis no use asking me now, Diarmid. He went and I never saw him again. He flew to the south and the Lord decreed our partnership should end. I cleaned up his house and when it was finished I came to Dunphilly. With his money I bought this house and I've tried to do what he would have liked. I've sent Sean to the college and then to Trinity; I've made a gentleman of him, for his good, and what does he do? Does he go for teacher, or a solicitor, or a dentist? He does not. He says, 'I'm going into the Air Force, Mother. I'm going to fly and get away from these parts. There's nothing to do here. Why don't you live in the city? You could have a house in Phoenix Park. There's nothing to do here but brood.' He's a boy to be doing, Diarmid, not like his father, or any of the O'Hallorans. A lazy lot, they are, paddling in their small acre, scratching a living from the soil. There are times when I think he's a changeling, when to punish me further he's been sent to despise me.

There's a lot of his grandfather in him, his Riall grandfather, and more of his English grandmother, she who lies on Clunare in a sheltered dell. There's no fear in him, Diarmid. He laughs at my fancies and says a woman faddles too much."

"They said — " he began.

"They did," said Kirsty, "and there was truth in their sayings, and a great black gulf of disaster. I found the lump when I was packing up Amos' clothes, as large as a gull's egg in my breast, and it was like going down to the hell of despair and dying with him. I carried it with me all the time I was there and after I had come to Dunphilly, feeling it grow and having no courage to withstand it. God had acted, as I had known He would. I was damned, and what could I do? Then another one came, in my arm, and it was agony to lift it. My flesh began to shrink and people said Kirsty O'Halloran was like to a ghost. Sean was away to the city, on his career. He was not yet old enough to leave. It became a battle, Diarmid, between staying for him and the cancer gnawing at my breast. I knew my adversary. I knew my fate. Kirsty O'Halloran had tempted the Lord and she was paying for her pride. She could not evade it or carry her head without fear.

"You'll not know the havoc of those days. You'll not know the fear of finding more lumps, of seeing the flesh fade, or looking at myself with sinking eyes, full of the revelation of my sin; the futility with which at last I crept to God and confessed my deeds, and the compassion of Doctor Costain. He was a true saint, that man. It was too deep for the cutting; I should have gone to him months before; he could only give me drugs, to lessen the pain. A true saint and one who understood the temptations of conceit. The counsellor Father O'Rourke was, but he was from me, leading me to confession, quoting the pangs of unrighteousness, and I found less gain in him than in Doctor Costain. That too was wrong. I was still a pagan, fighting for my hold on my child, defying the church, holding my gaze on the rough path when I should be sighting the cross.

"It was the end of the year and my time was fast coming. I had the wish to see Cloncobh and above all the beauty of the bay and Clunare. If I was to go, this time for ever, I might rest easier if I had seen that fair sight. They spoke of miracles on Clunare. All my life I had heard of them, the curing of ills by the good saint Cuimin. I had the thought too Padraig ought to know I was not well. I had no heart for his sympathy but I knew him at Marchmont, a man of books, nursing his grievances, through my brother Eamon who came to Dunphilly each week with hens for the market. Should I not try to repair the hurt I had done him? When one is ill, Diarmid, one looks at the world with different eyes. Amos had taught me tolerance and forbearance; we had talked of Padraig. I knew him alone. I could not go from this fair earth knowing there might be a word from me might make the way smoother for him and Sean. There might come a day he would like the voice of a son. I knew myself cut off but God wrought greater miracles and while I had strength I must try. I made them carry me to Cloncobh. I had Eamon bring his cart and wrap me in blankets and rugs and drive me along the high-banked roads, and a peace came, that evening, overriding the damp, the wet drizzle that layered my face. You would not have known me, Diarmid, so wasted like sticks; my friend Amos would have cried out for my helplessness; but in Cloncobh there was peace. I was going home. If I never came back, I should have known this contentment. I thought of nothing. Sean, Amos, Padraig, my brothers and sisters, my parents, even Cuimin and his shrine — all were in a haze, lost in the drug Doctor Costain had given me. 'Dear Mother of Mary,' I prayed, 'forgive me my past. I have sinned and I repent me of my sins.' It was the sudden clear period before death, they were to tell me, setting on my brow a touch of the Virgin, so that I smiled and never complained when the boat pitched and tossed and Pat O'Brien said we'd never get there. 'We shall,' I said. 'We shall see Cuimin, the great bard that he was, standing by his shrine in his homespun things.' I was convinced he would be there, and he was. I saw him Diarmid, a gentle man, with the brow of a scholar, standing by the crumbled altar — only then it was whole and about him was his church, built with his hands, and he had a book in his hand, and he said:

'Kirsty O'Halloran.' I said: 'I have come.'
He nodded. 'Do with me what you will,'
I said. 'I am finished with pride,' but he
shook his head gravely and was gracious
with me, the teacher with the pupil,
explaining, exhorting . . . There was no
pain; my limbs had taken on new strength;
my eyes could see over the island and the
bay and the gap between the Pins and the
Reek. 'Is it Marchmont I must go to?'
I asked. 'Must I swallow myself and go
to the stone house and say, Padraig Riall,
I am come — ?' He was reading his book
and when I would hasten, knowing them
waiting below, anxious for the result of
my madness, he reproved: 'The Lord will
provide.' I felt the deep faith all about me,
in the grass, in the stones, in the air that
rustled and shivered, and when I looked
again he was gone, the church was gone, and
I was kneeling on the bare, wet stones
with my head against the altar slab, but
his voice was there, in the cry of a gull,
in the sudden whimper of a gannet, the
movement of a leaf. 'The Lord will
provide.' Life or death, it was the Lord's.
And I rose from my knees and walked
down the path and my eyes were clear,

my carriage upright. I was full of the peace of that sacred place.

"As we went back a wind sprang up and rocked the boat and Donal said we should capsize and I smiled and said: 'We will swim, Donal. The Lord does not intend us to drown tonight'." She smiled faintly. "Poor, abstracted Donal. He was staring at me like one possessed. 'Your face, your body,' he said and I looked at my hands and they did not appear as wasted as they had. 'You're alight,' he said and could scarce speak for the awe. 'Alive,' I said, 'and with work to do.' He said it was a miracle. I had been carried to Clunare on a stretcher but now I was sitting up, speaking. Diarmid, ask me no questions. The fact is the proof. There was no cancer, Doctor Costain says, but my guiltiness making a martyr of me, insisting I had lumps in my breast, my arms, my neck. He knew; he had touched them; he knew the pain; he gave me the drugs; he was in perplexity, poor man, and we've let it be. We say Cuimin was there, in his holy church, as he always will be for those who seek him, who acknowledge his sainthood. You cannot deny . . ."

"If you saw him, Kirsty, I will take your word. I know my mother found peace and was content when she came from Clunare. Perhaps Padraig is right to protect the shrine."

"He is not! He has no right to refuse the holy comfort from those in pain." Vehemently, the refusal came out. "He is a blackleg, thinking to banish the sun . . ." She went on more calmly: "I came off the boat and Padraig was there, sent by Cuimin to greet me . . . Diarmid, I'll never forget his virulence, his icy scorn. I said: 'God has forgiven us. He has given me light,' and . . . You know his reply? He told you?"

"I am ashamed for my brother," said Diarmid. "He is not himself."

"He is foolish," said Kirsty, "to refuse the light that shone blindingly on Clunare."

"He is suffering."

"God makes His erring sons to suffer. It is right and proper that Padraig should suffer, even unto death."

"Kirsty," he said, "you did not meet Nemesis on Clunare; you learned humility and faith and a great easing of spirit. That night you forgave yourself and Padraig all your hurts. That he tossed your advance in your face makes no difference at all. He is the one to whom you gave . . ."

"He is nothing to me."

"You will not help me to cure him?"

"Can Padraig Riall be cured?"

"Kirsty O'Halloran was cured of a cancer," said Diarmid deliberately.

"Go away," she said harshly. "Go back to England and your designing and your artist friends and leave us alone here in Dunphilly. I have found ease. I have a house and a son, and employment when I need it. Scoff, Diarmid, if you will, but Kirsty O'Halloran is still the finest housekeeper in these parts."

He met her brittle gaze. "Would you ever consider coming to be my housekeeper?"

"For shame," she exclaimed, "have I bared my soul to be taken in joke by a Riall? Get thee gone, son of a Philistine."

He laughed. "So you can still flash, you lovely woman. Would you sell that portrait? To my friend, Lewis Hope? He's a connoisseur."

"I will not."

"I thought not." He rose and went to it and studied it. "It's a beautiful thing," he repeated, "one of the finest Amos ever did."

"You'll not have it."

He agreed. "No, Kirsty, it should remain with you, the memorial to a unique relationship. Thank you for telling me your story. You need not have done so, though I am your brother-in-law strangely. When Sean is in London, tell him to call on me. He will be — what? Twenty-two? The sad, sorry thick-head, Padraig is, to have a son and not know him. I'll tell him, the . . . Kirsty, I'll not belittle your confidence, but Padraig is sick; he has these blurred moods; if he were not who he is, would you not raise a hand to help, you who have spoken with Cuimin?" He had the magic of pleading in his soft Irish voice and she moved impatiently. "The fact remains you are the one who best knows— I shall not be long at Marchmont. Jeremy Crooke will be after me, for the décor for *The Irish Room*. And Hector Burne will write me, in that take-no-refusal way." A sudden idea had occurred to him. "I know your address and I shall write to you. Don't toss my letter in the basket. Russell Landon lives in Amos' old house. I've been there often. Next time I go I'll imagine you there, the correct young housekeeper with the unofficial body. It's a fine body, Kirsty. Russell would delight in it."

"I'm not for sale," tartly.

"You never were. That's why Padraig never really held you. Always the O'Halloran stock contested the bargain. I'm a wiser man than I was."

"You're still a Riall."

"A foreign Riall. Did you know my mother ?"

" 'Tis a bewitcher you are, Diarmid Riall. I'll not talk with you any more. You've stolen my morning and I was due at the convent to give the girls a lesson in housewifery. I'll do it," she said, "whatever you say. I have my way and you have yours — "

"And if they should touch at odd moments I'll be thankful to St. Cuimin," he said. "I'm beginning to find the old saint an obliging religious."

7

HE had spent the morning in the library with *The Irish Room*. Hearing a step, he glanced round. "Come in, Father," he invited. What about putting this rural priest into Hector's scenes, casting him for Father Flaherty? It was an enticing thought but could it be? "I needed space," sweeping his hand over the sheets of folio spread on the desk. "I'm experimenting at the moment. Are you usually offered hospitality?"

"There's nothing to touch Fingal's Nine," said Father O'Rourke. He bent his head over the largest sheet of paper.

"You recognise it?"

"I see you were admitted."

"I shall need her permission to use it," said Diarmid. "I'm full of feelings about Kirsty O'Halloran, Father."

"She's an extraordinary woman," taking the glass.

"In that she sinned and repented?"

"In that she shared with the rest of us the weaknesses of mankind."

"I hope I never have to suffer her torments," replied Diarmid. "She was frank with me, after a hesitant beginning. I'd like you to know that."

"I'm surprised she let you in."

"I said I was her brother-in-law," simply.

The other's brows came together. "She saw you, with that?"

"She may have heard my name and been consumed with curiosity. I find most people very credulous, Father. As it turned out, I had been to the house in London where she spent a number of years. I knew Amos Brierley's work. My greatest friend is an art dealer. I know Russell Landon who lives there now. I scarcely expected to find a connection between artistic circles in London and a small town in Co. W— but as you say, life is full of coincidences. Would you say there was a design indicated, Father?"

The long, dark robe in the shaft of sunshine which came in through the mullioned window showed patches of mould where it had lain in the presbytery, or been flung carelessly over a chair.

"To teach us our place in the world?"

he went on. "I am floundering, I admit. I require Hector's unbiased mind to sift these rum fallacies. I'll away to London, to brood at my leisure."

The priest was smiling. He put his empty glass on the desk.

"We have rather smothered you with rumness, have we not? 'Tis a way we have in Co. W—. We are jealous of our characteristics."

"I didn't ask to be smothered."

"You did not, and I ask you to be patient. More than a dig is on hand, as you will have gleaned; more than the isolating of Cuimin's island . . ."

"That's incidental, surely. It never has been isolated, except by the tides. I wouldn't cut it off any more than I'd burn down Marchmont. It's the way of nature to be contrary and the duty of us all, surely, to attune ourselves to its demands, to go the way that we feel is the right one. This dig could be the saving of so much. You needn't hide the truth from me, Father. You fear that if Padraig goes on as he is he'll lose hold. If he could give himself some cause, some sound purpose . . . He wouldn't come to London, I suppose? He hasn't some latent talent we could encourage. Marcia might arrange an interview with Sir Bruno. He hasn't had any training beyond that year as a wage-earner. This place deadens the wits; it clamps an iron band on the cultivation of ideas; it's not so much evil as desultory."

"Saint Cuimin chose it, from all Ireland," murmured Father O'Rourke.

"We are not Saint Cuimin. We are men and women living in the twentieth century when discoveries pronounce daily some feverish advance towards annihilation. What, I ask you, would St. Cuimin have made of nuclear warfare?"

"The same as he made of elemental frustration."

"All right." He conceded the point. "Tell me, this boy of Kirsty's?"

"Like all boys. At the moment away to the far side of the world in a flying machine."

Diarmid chuckled. There was little in Cloncobh that was in touch with up-to-date machinery, save the diabolical inventions of men's minds. Would Sean O'Halloran accept complacently the calling of his RAF Valiant a "flying machine"? He moved to the window overlooking the garden. Beyond the railings dividing it from Quilty's Pasture, he could see the scattered figures of the dig. Which, of all those heads, was Marcia's? What was she making of this visit to Marchmont?

"Time presses, alas. Give the Professor my apologies and say I am busy designing an Irish room. I believe he has hopes of finding the extent of the abbot's lodging today. He was abnormally excited at breakfast time."

He continued working, his pencil flying over the paper, the paint pot changing colour rapidly. Mrs. Sullivan brought his coffee and he drank it hot, his mind choked with conjectures. It was the room of the house in Stephen's Green that Hector had chosen. With luck he would have something to offer by tomorrow and then, if Jeremy came . . . Often, he had second or third thoughts but not this time. It was to be this room or not at all.

"No, I have not seen Padraig. He is away to Clunare, Mrs. Sullivan says, seeking the book Kirsty saw in Cuimin's hand." Father O'Rourke was back, standing in the doorway. "Was there really a book of Cuimin? I shall know when Padraig returns."

The wind that had risen in late afternoon and rushed gustily round the house had scampered away so that now the murmurs were friendly and small. Padraig must have had a dangerous time in the bay and the saint had not lifted a hand to direct him when the skiff got out of control. The clouds had been lowcast over the island. At five o'clock Marcia had said: "I hope Mr. Riall's not afloat at this moment." There was nothing to confirm or deny the uneasy suspicions, save the shocked look on Padraig's face, the flexing and gripping of the fingers indicative of straining at oars, the stiffness with which he went up the stairs after dinner.

Diarmid escaped to the terrace.

"May I intrude?"

He turned. "I'm wishing I had never come," he confessed.

"You're too near." She came to his side. "What particularly is nagging you?"

"The fear . . . He was out in the bay this afternoon. He got ashore, certainly, but he hasn't said . . . apart from the fact that he got wet and he's tired. I'm not thinking it . . . I don't for a moment believe he intended . . . He went to find the book."

"You're imagining," she said. "A woman's hallucination?"

"Maybe."

"When I leave here," she said, "you must come to Winter's Grace."

Involuntarily: "What a delightful name."

"My father's house in Surrey."

"I shan't have another holiday for months. Once I'm back my life will be one whirl of instructions."

"I don't believe it," stoutly. "Diarmid Riall can hold his own."

"The whims of the art world are predictable. It's the whims of Irish saints . . ."

"What you want," prosaically, "is an attack by the Danes."

"I shall probably have it, in the shape of Jeremy Crooke."

"I'm looking forward to meeting the gentleman."

"Marcia," he turned and regarded her, "do you think Padraig should — go away?"

The moonlight showed the various heaps of the dig, resembling sleeping animals dotted about the sward.

"You mean — ?"

"Dublin or London; somewhere not this side of Ireland."

"Would he respond?"

"I haven't a notion. His only travels beyond Marchmont have been ill-fated. If he went and saw where Kirsty had lived . . ."

"You're pinning too much on Kirsty."

He shrugged. "It all began with Kirsty. She's there, a woman to love, as you said. I had an hour with her. I envy Amos Brierley . . . You did not know?" He told her, adding what he himself had known of the painter.

"Diarmid, how sad!"

"Sad and beautiful. He was the means of awaking her womanhood, giving her poise."

"Nevertheless, you're making too much of her," she insisted. "You mustn't mind me, Diarmid. I'm on the outside, a spectator. You're putting her on a pedestal and consigning Padraig to outer darkness."

"I told him he should be ashamed of himself."

"Before you saw her. To be blunt, she's a fallen woman. She lived with Amos Brierley."

"As his housekeeper," promptly.

"Diarmid! He loved her."

"I could love her myself."

She shook her head wonderingly. "Is that it? Has she cast her spell on you now? Your brother was a boy, refused his own home; you're a man, on a pinnacle of fame. What is there, in an O'Halloran, that can affect two such opposites?"

He acknowledged her wisdom. "I told you I needed your clarity. I have no shame. Kirsty O'Halloran is a woman to love. Go and see her and tell her I sent you."

"Would she welcome me?"

"Because she is what she is, she would; because she has passed through the valley of death."

"She really had the cancer?"

"She had a cancer. She knelt at St. Cuimin's altar and was healed."

She shook her head. "It's no good, Diarmid. It's beyond me."

"You wouldn't be telling me you don't believe in Cuimin?" he enquired.

"There you have the advantage, though so far there's no proof. I'd hate to say so to the Professor but he's very likely on the wrong line. This may not be St. Cuimin's abbey at all."

"Whose then?"

She quoted several saints. "All were hereabouts during the early years of Christianity."

"Next you'll be telling me he never lived on Clunare."

"Did he live on Clunare?"

"The legend is over a thousand years old. Would I be brave enough to say a saint was created, not in fact, but in the fabrication of local minds? Cuimin lived on Clunare. He may have lived here. If it is of assistance to Padraig, let him have lived here. I hate to see him as he is . . . You haven't helped me much."

"My father knows Sir Eric Frost."

"Would he come here?"

"He prefers his patients to go to him. Might it not be better, away from Marchmont? There is this contagiousness about it."

"Nearly drowning yourself in Clunare Bay is not a flight of the imagination," tersely.

"You can't say that." She shivered, nevertheless. In her heart she was convinced. The owner of Marchmont had almost foundered and St. Cuimin had let him wallow. Nonsense! She was as bad as the natives. Close to antiquity as she was, she was not ridden by ancient lore. Runes, to her, meant not some antiquated mysticism but the writings of men who lived centuries before. Burial grounds of chieftains proved the corpses had been fact, not the formulating of vague legends and tales that made people stay in at night. "He did not drown," she said prosaically, "and if we stay here any longer we shall get influenza. Don't say the saint will protect us. He won't."

He chuckled amusedly. "Mrs. Sullivan would cure us," he replied. "On my way home I'll enquire about the nursing homes."

"Why not ask Kirsty O'Halloran?"

What possessed her to say that, snapping the remark at him spitefully? The sudden turmoil of her heart astounded her, frightened her. She had known him three days and in another three days he would be gone. She was aware of her torrential emotions, her lack of normal composure; the uneasiness showed in her knife-like retort. But he took it calmly, though thoughtfully, with concern.

"That's an idea. Thank you, Marcia. I will."

She was sitting on a knoll, going through the Professor's dictation, when a shout came from the direction of the abbot's house. A few more yards of wall had been unearthed, unhewn slabs of rocks taken bodily from the Reek. She looked up, held by the urgency.

"Where's the Prof.?" One of the team came pounding towards her.

"In the house. What is it? Have you found something?" She was on her feet, lithe as a gazelle.

"A small bundle." His dirt-streaked face was shining with excitement. "Charles unearthed it, between two stones. We haven't touched it."

"Go and fetch the Prof." Marcia was down in the excavated trench, joining the cluster of diggers. On a heap of earth lay a discoloured roll of canvas or hemp or parchment; it was almost impossible to decide of what material. It might be nothing . . . or everything. She remembered similar finds in Corfu. A palimpsest of the Middle Ages. As it was touched it fell to pieces and only fragments remained. "Don't touch it," with authority.

"It fell out when I disturbed that stone."

She was on her knees, pushing her hand into a cavity. "It was probably a small cupboard where the abbot kept his records. I hope the Prof. hasn't gone to Dunphilly."

"Here he comes."

"What is it, Marcia?" Codrill was beside her, bending his white head over the discoloured bundle, lifting it with a pair of tweezers he took from his pocket. "Well done," he said. "This should give us proof. Have you a sheet of paper?"

She pulled one from her notebook and watched breathlessly as he laid the find on it.

"This is wonderful," he cried. His thin, pale face was alight with his joy.

"What is it?" she asked. "A record of payments, a list of duties, a book of prayer? Paulinus? Palladius?" It was too recent for Cuimin yet an anticipation tingled her blood. If it could be Cuimin's . . .

"Find Mr. Riall. Say I'm going to the library. He would want it there." He hurried across the pasture, bearing the precious bundle, not more than three inches long, but as valuable to him as a declaration of rights. "Come with me, Marcia. I may require written record. Your eyes are clearer than mine." He blinked in the radiant sunshine.

Following him, she yet had time to catch a glimpse of Clunare, standing up clear and sharp between the Pins and the Reek. For the second time in a week, the isle was free, showing them Christianity's first stronghold. Was that an omen? She accompanied Alec Codrill into the house.

It was a list of the abbots since Cuimin's arrival. Some they could decipher; the onset of time and the damp of the moist peat soil had moulded the original parchment; blotched patches and stains had destroyed the script of some long-buried monk; but the first names were readable. Whoever had rolled the record had rolled the top into the middle. The final wording was impossible to read.

"It looks like a D," Marcia said.

"Donatus," said Padraig. He was bending over the scroll, a magnifying glass in his fingers. The scholar was uppermost. Diarmid's right, she thought; he needs impetus,

174

a task of great magnitude, to cull the knowledge he had amassed in solitary study. Too much solitude had come near to driving an inward nature on to tragedy, so that now when he had others with him he shied, unable to direct his allegiance. "He was much earlier. 987." His voice was authoritative. "Deodatus was — " He frowned. "1190. 1192. Eleven hundred and ninety. In that decade."

"It's not Deodatus," said Marcia. "There's not enough space for that."

"Damian," said Padraig. "1164. There have been Damians in Cloncobh since the thirteenth century. There is a stone in the churchyard to a Damian O'Dea. And a Damian O'Finn, and a Damian Coyle."

"Isn't there a Damian O'Halloran?" Codrill asked. "A young fellow with a lorry? I've seen him going round with the peat."

"Damian O'Halloran died in '35," snapped Padraig. "Like his daughter, he is gone."

"I don't expect they've bothered to paint the name out," laughed Marcia. "Your young man's name is Eamon. He came to the dig once."

"I'll have no O'Halloran on my land,"

hoarsely. Padraig's eyes burned in their sockets.

"He hasn't been since." Dear Lord, how he hated the O'Hallorans. "It must be Damian." She gave her attention to the roll. "That's five in a row then. Patricius. Olricus. Destinius. Malachius. Damianus. The beginning is a lot clearer." She bent nearer. "Donatus. Ericus. Cuthbertus. When was Cuthbertus abbot, Mr. Riall?"

"889. Can you read them clearly?" He leaned further over the desk. "Can you see, Codrill? P-A-T-R-I-C-I-U-S. The saint. Then O-L-R-I-C-U-S. You realise what this is?"

"A record of the abbots of Cuimin's abbey from the middle of the ninth century. An intensely valuable document, Mr. Riall. It must be preserved."

"You have no doubt?"

"Well, yes," Codrill admitted. "There must be doubts until the scroll has been verified. I'll write to Professor Termion at Trinity and ask him to put arrangements in hand to have it under test."

"Unless Mr. Riall would like to take it to Trinity himself."

"Trinity? This should go to London, to

the British Museum. You understand, sir, the importance of this find. The scroll must be treated. Miss French's eyes are good but under giant magnifying glasses and special processes we shall be permanently sure of its value. I'd estimate in the nature of five thousand pounds, judging by the figures put on other medieval antiquities."

"It's incomplete," put in Padraig. "We need another scroll from Cuimin to Cuthbert."

The professor was like a man rejuvenated. "Never fear, Mr. Riall. We shall intensify our efforts. Now we know that we are on the right track we shall not rest until we have unearthed whatever lies hidden. That is, of course, if you are prepared to put up with us for another period of months."

The dig was a fury of activity. Word had gone round about the discovery and men from the neighbouring villages had come to gape and gesture. The Professor had telephoned to Dublin and an authority was on his way to verify the manuscript.

"If only we could find the other half," Marcia said, "his cup would be full."

"If only — " Diarmid teased. "If only St. Cuimin would come over from Clunare and tell us where to look."

"Well, tell him," sharply. She was trying vainly to keep the Professor free of the pressing crowds. "We might then return to our previous peace."

"Don't you like notoriety? I find it refreshing."

"Padraig doesn't."

"No. Poor old chap. I suppose it's not funny, having your domain invaded. All right. I'll rescue him. I'll take him to Clunare to look for the lost shamrock."

"What lost shamrock?"

"Didn't you know? The sheep eat it as fast as it grows."

"Oh, be quiet!"

He grinned. "I didn't have time to find it the last time I was there. Donal only gave me half an hour."

"What's the matter with you?" tersely.

"I'm under the influence." Actually, he had had a long letter from Lewis Hope. "I'm chasing an early Landon for Sir Bruno Waldstein. Do you know him? He's a big-wig in the City. The next Lord Mayor, so I hear." It was satisfying to have known before Lewis. He'd make the old chap open his eyes when he told him he knew, not Sir Bruno personally, though he hoped soon to make his acquaintance, at Winter's Grace in Surrey, but Sir Bruno's daughter, a young lady by the name of Marcia French, actual daughter, so Codrill had told him, of Valentine French, the writer, who had been killed with his wife on the Upper Corniche above Nice. Codrill had told him much in snippets and oddments.

Lewis would enjoy his new chase. He had a nose for ferreting out information and unearthing valuable paintings. Look at his flair for the Braydons which had "made him" in Milsom Street.

Begorra, he thought, it was good to have a friend like Lewis. When he was back in England, he would tell him about the dig and value his opinion.

But he had said he would rescue Padraig. He touched him on the elbow.

"I'm going to Clunare. Will you show me what you found the other day? I haven't much more time. Jeremy will descend . . . and I'd like to think we had a few hours together on its mound."

When they were on the shore and had commandeered Donal Murphy's boat: "You row," said Diarmid, pushing it down to the water's edge. "I remember in the old days you always rowed, being the older, and I took the helm. There were no engines then. We'll not have the engine now. The sea's calm and the sky's blue." He settled himself firmly into the stern. The waves lapped the side of the boat. "What greater inspiration could any man want than this delectable coast? A symphony could be composed here, based on the coming of Cuimin. You know no music? I'm not ignorant but there's no time. We'd want a Reed or a Morse to catch this tonal power. There's not many men could encase it. Lefaille might, but he tends to over-exaggerate. There's such reflection in water, such miracles that the heart halts, too breathless for words." His sibilant voice ran on, easing the other over a further crossing to Clunare. It was one reason why he had brought him, to satisfy himself he could leave him, not have a summons almost as soon as he had gone, to take a dripping body from the sea. He wished he could plumb the inquietude in Padraig.

Doctor Costain had tried; Father O'Rourke was trying; in their way, Alec Codrill and Marcia were willing to help; but the degree of the sting lay in Kirsty O'Halloran. He could not bring her to Marchmont and confront Padraig with her; he had considered it and rejected it; it was too redundant of danger; Padraig would do one of two things: fly into a temper or retreat into a jaundice, neither of which did Diarmid wish to discern. Nor could he take him to the house in Dunphilly and say: "She is there, my brother; she awaits you, with the love of the ordained . . ." Instead, he had brought him to Clunare, in the hope that it would check the dark virus before it spread further.

Watching him now, rowing strongly, with the swing of the born waterman, he was sure some storm had overtaken Padraig the other afternoon, making a mockery of seamanship. Suddenly he wondered, had Padraig convinced himself he was in their mother's case, there was nothing curable in the malaise that had settled on him, that in fact a canker or cancer was eating into his limbs? The island was near. They were on the other side of the sun. Lying beneath the cliffs, the water was turbid, impenetrable. Serpents and slugs could lurk there . . .

"Have you told Superintendent Mulligan of the find? I didn't see him in the pasture with the others."

"He's away to Kilmeenan on a corruption case."

"He'll see in it a lightening of his labours." Diarmid reached out to clutch the rough rock beside the upward path. "I have it. Secure the painter. Have you done it? Alanna, what's up?"

"A piece of seaweed." Padraig hastily recovered himself but he was shaken. "I did not see it." Bending, he tossed the weed into the sea.

"I never knew seaweed on Clunare." Diarmid jumped out lithely and tested the thoroughness of the rope's fastening. "I'd not like to swim to shore at that."

"The tides change," said Padraig. He was waiting impatiently.

"Sending little whirlpools into Cuimin's paradise?" Beginning to climb, he was aware of Padraig behind him, nasally panting. There was something wrong then? Some strain? Maybe, the effect of im-

182

mersion in the sea? "Cuimin chose well when he alighted on this place. I pity the Danes trying to pry him from his fastness." He breasted the rise and the serenity and peace of the valley caught him afresh. For a second he paused, content to gaze. Then he went onward, towards the ruined church and the broken altar before which Kirsty had knelt and been reborn.

"He was reading a book," Kirsty had said in her warm, mellow voice. "The peace of the holy place was all around me."

"*He was reading a book.*" Cuimin had been a great scholar, writing down the beliefs that threshed and gathered within him. The first of the saints. He enumerated them, in a soft, pliant murmur, wondering idly where the other scroll might be, offering a prayer to Cuimin that he might reveal it to them.

"Diarmid!"

Padraig was on the other side of the dell, looking down at a stone almost covered in gorse and lichen, scarred by the weather.

"Is it hers?" Diarmid covered the intervening distance and scratched away the moss, seeking the name, but the stone was bare. He looked up interrogatively.

"He let it be — ? Why have you, if you knew it here — ?" Sharply, of a sudden, a spurious anger whipped up in him. "You were the guardian of Marchmont and Clunare. Had you no thought or no mind to perpetuate her resting place? Had you such selfishness — ?" Then the fever was gone. What better place for a beloved soul to lie? Who greater or more forbearing than St. Cuimin himself? Had there been a title visitors would have defaced it, gorging curiously on a Riall who was not buried in the churchyard. As it was, she was in far holier ground . . . "You were right," he admitted; he let the moss drop back. "Some people do not need the limelight or the glare. I shall know where she is and have no more aches. I could not have chosen a fairer spot." He watched a gull hover gracefully over the broken altar. "If I should die," he mused, "before I come to my allotted span, you can lie me here, with her, in this pleasant dell . . ." but his brother had gone, to the altar, ten paces away, staring down at the jumbled stones, bending to touch one and to hold it in his fingers . . . Ah, the lost boyeen . . .

The sudden cry startled him. Padraig

was stumbling over the rough, uneven ground.

"What is it?"

"It's here, Diarmid. I've found it. In a crevice." His sunken cheeks were quivering.

"What is? Cuimin's book?"

"A package like the other, wedged into a crack." His hands were bleeding from the energy expended; the nails were torn.

"Steady," said Diarmid. '*He was reading a book*', Kirsty said. An importunate thought raced like the wind. With Cuimin's book, might there not come an explanation, a lessening of the gulf between two people who had once been one? "Let's do it carefully. Take down these stones."

It was easy to say, less easy to do. In thirty minutes no more than a small hole had been worked.

"We must come back," said Diarmid. "We need tools. Wait! The crowbar in the boat. I'll fetch it."

He ran down the winding path. Proof of Cuimin's ministry? It would cause a stir beyond Marchmont. Cuimin was a local saint, barely known in the outer world, but with definite proof . . . He laughed exultantly. "Your imagination runs away with you" — Aunt Ma-Ma's cry. He felt like leaping from land to sky and back again.

The crowbar was useful. With it they prised out the rough stones and revealed the small cavity beyond. The brown package fell with a plop at Padraig's feet.

"Handle it carefully," ordered Diarmid. "The other part of the list? Gently, Padraig. What's that? Decimus? The twelfth? Did he come before Cuthbert? Then it is the other half. Snug and safe all these years, placed here probably by Decimus himself. Clunare keeps herself to herself when the winds howl. But by the time of Cuthbert men had learned to laugh at the wind, thought to know how to handle the waves, so they left it, and the abbey crumbled about it, until Codrill ferreted it out? 'Tis a story fit to swell the heart of an Irishman. Proud, I am, to have a part in it. We'll take it to Codrill and lay it out on the table beside the other, and get the magnifying lenses to it, and trace the full line." A sudden fear gnawed like a rat. "I suppose it is the full line, Padraig. Lie it on the slab. Look! Decimus. Clodus. Destinius.

Marcus. I've heard of Marcus. Something our father once said."

"He landed on Clunare and built a settlement in Cuimin's name."

"How can that be, if Cuimin him-self — ?"

"They were driven back in 790, to retreat to the mother church."

"Johannus. Minimus. Josephus. Paulinius. Palladius. Adrianus. We must be near the beginning, surely. Cedricus. Cuiminus. The first name, clear and bold, as that early chronicler wrote it. Padraig, it takes the words from one's lips. Cuiminus. Cedricus. Adrianus. Down to Decimus. You can open the abbey at the Royal and preserve these two pieces of parchment, but should you? Clunare has always been here, for those who sought it. Cuimin would not have his altar removed. It's for you to decide," but Padraig was already on the way down to the boat, bearing the package. Diarmid took one look at the ruins. Then he bent to replace a few of the stones.

"We've added to the desolation, Cuimin. We'll repair it for you. I'll return with trowel and mortar."

His eye caught a dark object lying

amongst the stones. As he took it up, inquisitively, he saw it was a book, very small, written in hand, with illuminations faint and blotched beside the initial letters. A book . . . '*He was reading a book*', said Kirsty. Could it be? Another miracle, to aid them in their wonderings? The actual volume which the saint had used? Mother of God, it was far more precious, far more valuable than any medieval tome; it must be placed in a strong place where all the world could see it.

He opened it hesitantly, fearing for its safety, lest it crumble in his hands and fade from view . . . and saw the word "Cuiminus" on the fly-leaf, and knew he was with a treasure. "*I am with God . . .*" Painstakingly, he translated the Latin, marred though it was by the ravages of time. "*The Lord's word . . .*"

After what seemed aeons, though was in fact only a few moments, he went down the path to the boat. Padraig was sitting with the oars.

"I've found the greatest thing on earth. Cuimin's own book," and he gave it wordlessly to his brother.

PART TWO

THE BOOK

1

THE Book of Cuimin was on show in the library of St. Cuimin's College in Dunphilly. It had been to Dublin and to London and professors of antiquity and divinity had pored over its Latin phrases, and pronounced it genuine. It had been valued at ten thousand pounds, *pro tem*, there being no other to compare it with, and returned to Padraig reluctantly and with reverence. Trinity College had wanted to place it in the Golden Room beside the Book of Kells; the British Museum fought hard for its retention; but Padraig said, and there were plenty of his countrymen to uphold him, that it should remain in St. Cuimin's country and by that he meant Marchmont or possibly Dunphilly. He was not averse to Dunphilly, that part of it occupied by the college, where he had spent many rewarding hours with Seamus Macroom, delving into the Celtic lore, and carried it one day in its special protective covering to hand over to the old man.

" 'Tis better here, Seamus," he announced. "The crowds are undoing me."

"Och!" agreed Seamus. He indicated the glass-covered stand ready to receive the treasure. "I'll not mind the crowds either but it is the college that will be benefiting. The good saint will remember you, Padraig Riall, for seeing that his Book is properly housed. And 'tis more people can be seeing it here and enjoying its writings, and dropping an offering in the box, betimes." His acquisitive eyes shone like bright sunshine on Finneboyle Lough. "For sure, Padraig, the Principal will be thanking you for your generosity and remembering you in his orations."

The Book was placed in its new home, the tenderness and care with which Seamus held it being indicative of his wordless worship; then the key was turned in the lock after the name card was in place. "The Book of Cuimin, est. 541. Written and used by St. Cuimin and discovered on Clunare on 25th August 1962." An odd one, thought Seamus, shaking his greying head, as Padraig went out of the library. A pity he wouldn't let the love take possession of him and govern his ways. A pity, a pity, a pity, indeed.

"I am learning the Latin," wrote Kirsty. "It takes up a good deal of my day, preparing my exercises for the evening when I go to the Old Library and sit with Seamus Macroom. He is a dear, kind, patient man, which is to the good, for I am not the best of scholars, having had few teachers: Padraig when we were in Dublin and he could be persuaded to teach me my letters, Mrs. Shane in a fit of indulgence, thinking to fashion me to a personal maid, Amos when we were together in the house in Roxhall Gardens. Have you been to the house yet? You wrote me you were paying a visit to Russell Landon. I have a great jealousy of the man, being in Amos' studio. Not until you write to say he is using it kindly will I know any relief from the gnawing inside me. I am full of these gnawings. They are the result of you badgering me. Before you came, that day in the summer, before the finding of the lists and the Book of Cuimin, I was at home with myself. I could walk in the street and see him, for sure and have no feelings of pity, but now . . . He has had a visitor at Marchmont. The diggers have departed for the winter and this man came. A specialist from London, said Seamus, or was it from Dublin? Little goes on in Dunphilly; when it does the disturbing is like a storm over Finneboyle Lough. A tall, distinguished gentleman, I am told, who was on a walking tour, and who unfortunately sprained his ankle at the entrance to Marchmont. 'Come in,' says Padraig. 'Mrs. Sullivan will tie it up.' Och, it was nothing, says the other. He would get to the hotel. Was there a hotel? You can picture them, Diarmid, arguing and protesting and it beginning to rain, pelting down as it does while they debated the niceties of hospitality. 'Go your way then,' said Padraig. 'Marchmont is a poor house.' 'Marchmont?' says the other. 'Have I not heard of Marchmont? A discovery of some kind?' He limps beside Padraig. 'A discovery of great moment?' 'It's at Dunphilly,' says

Padraig. 'Go there. A book, the oldest book in the land. You'll have to steal it; it's padlocked and battened down and protected by an old old man named Macroom. You'll find the species all over Ireland. Libraries filled with them, whereas Rialls . . .' You know how he enlarges on the Rialls. It's become a fetish with him. He must turn up the history to prove his antiquity."

Diarmid chuckled. The telephone on his desk rang shrilly and with one hand he took it up. "Hello," he said absently. The other was holding Kirsty's letter. So Sir Eric Frost had reached Marchmont and stayed. Soon, he would have his opinion.

"It's Marcia," said the telephone.

"Hallo," he said again.

"Are you coming to Winter's Grace this weekend?"

"If I may."

"You know I invited you. What's the matter with you?"

"Overwork. Hector. Jeremy. Your father. Lewis. Russell Landon."

"Has he found the picture?"

"He has not. It went to America in 1947. The man will not sell, not even for Sir

Bruno Waldstein, Lord Mayor elect. That's deflating for his worship. Landon's pulled out another. Even earlier, 1926 or thereabouts. When Lewis comes back from the Hague . . ."

"You're like will-o'-the-wisps, you two. I've been trying to get you for days."

"I've been to Cheshire. The Duchess of Radford wants me to 'do' her daughter's coming-of-age. Fabulous," he reported. "You'd never credit the oodles."

"Tell me when you see me. How will you come?"

"In Jeremy's Jaguar. He's in bed with a cold. Hence my abstraction. He's on the phone every few moments, wanting me at his flat. What with Jeremy and Hector, I'm pretty well at my wits' end."

"You'll cope," she opined. "What's amusing you?" alertly. "You sound agog despite your preoccupation."

"Kirsty," he told her. "She's learning the Latin."

"What did you say? The line's crackling so badly."

"That's the holy saints splitting their sides."

"Diarmid, be sensible!"

"I am sensible. Just a bit afraid too. Kirsty learning the Latin is not the Kirsty I know. She'll be changing herself, I'll be thinking."

"Drat Kirsty," said Marcia. "That woman has put a spell over you."

"She tells me Sir Eric Frost arrived with a sprained ankle and enjoyed a week of Padraig's hospitality."

"She's spiteful. It probably went off quite all right."

"Kirsty's not spiteful. It's you who spit. When's your next dig?"

"In a month from now. In Africa. Now, who's jealous?"

"Clarrie Throssell wants a Muslim setting. 'Tis kind to me the fates always are. Hector wishes an Irish setting and I go to the Royal. The Lord Mayor's thinking of employing me and you're squatting happily on a Cuimin dig."

"It was I who recommended you to Father," she reminded him.

"It matters not. I've got the job. It's doing nicely," he said. "I hope you've arranged about my ticket for the banquet. Beside you, my sweet Marcia."

There was a click and a crackle. "You're

all the same, you Irish. What else does Kirsty say?"

"I haven't read. You interrupted me. Shall I be ringing you later to continue your education? Chester's hovering in the doorway with a client."

"We haven't arranged — " she began.

"If you will bury yourself in Surrey, you mustn't be peeved if I take my pleasures elsewhere. It's you, Lewis?" replacing the receiver. "When did you return? Successful trip?" He swept aside his pile of papers. The letter from Kirsty he put in his pocket. "Mora well? I'm a god-father, remember."

Lewis Hope took a seat on a high stool. He was a broad-shouldered, sturdy man with the strong characteristics of the Mideans, though the banker Reuben had been his great-great-grandfather.

"Aunt Leah's coming to town. She has appointments and she'll remain. She's coming to *The Irish Room*."

"Everybody's coming to *The Irish Room*," said Diarmid. "The theatre won't be big enough to hold the people. Hector said Jeremy should have had the Meridian but you can't tell a Crooke — or hook."

He ran his hand through his thick dark hair. "I've never been so busy."

Lewis congratulated him. "I found my Nuysmans."

"Reasonable?"

"Twenty pounds apiece."

"Twenty . . . Lewis, you old twister! How do you do it? One look from those tigerish eyes. No wonder you outwitted the Vatican Palace."

"One inmate of the Vatican," corrected Lewis. The reference was in connection with his time in Venice when he sought a lamp from Murano and had his way barred by a Father Tomas, actually a scion of an old Venetian family. "It took more than looks to plumb his wiles. James Kaffer will pay a hundred willingly."

"With that Adam must retire at last."

Lewis smiled. "He grunts and expresses delight and comes in twice a week and nurses his heart and wishes he had married Aunt Leah. He doesn't say so, no. He will never acknowledge his error, the infallible Adam Greuzer."

Diarmid remarked gravely: "If men would only admit their mistakes, they would save us others a basinful of care."

"Who now?"

"I'm just expecting it, that's all, but you don't visit me so often that I can fill you with my woes. Is it a christening piece you'll be wanting, or a setting for your next exhibition, or a nursery redecorating? Prices are strictly net, Mr. 'Greuzer' Hope."

They bantered with the camaraderie of old friends. "I'm on my way to Landon," said Lewis. "If it's convenient, I thought you might accompany me."

"Nothing better." He jumped up. "I've had a letter from Kirsty O'Halloran. I was reading it when Marcia rang just before you appeared." They went down the stairs. "I'm going with Mr. Hope, Chester. I shall be about an hour. Take any messages that come."

"That's very good, Diarmid," said Lewis. He was inspecting the work in the lower workshop.

"Sir Bruno's impressed," at his elbow. "He came in the other day. I like him, Lewis. There's a quality about him that goes straight to the point."

Lewis nodded. "A contemporary of Reuben. No, not actually. In manners and accomplishment. I've been sounding my father for you. He's highly respected. Clever, of course; that goes without saying; and lucky. Everything he touches turns to gold."

"He'll have a baronetcy after his year?"

"Father expects him to be a baron in five years."

"Baron Waldstein of Winter's Grace."

"No. Baron Childwell in the county of Surrey."

"Trust the Jews," chanted Diarmid. He propelled Lewis out into the passageway. "We have the Greuzer car? After you, my lord."

"Are you worred, Diarmid?"

"Vaguely, yes. There's a funny feeling in my tummy . . ."

"When you hear the furore that design is going to cause, you'll forget your precious tummy."

"I'll be pleased when *The Irish Room* is on. The play's bedevilled. Jeremy's ill. Hector's on spikes. It only needs him to go down, and May Germaine to be snaffled by another producer, for the whole caboosh to go phut! It's a good play too, the best Hector's done."

"You've had your attention diverted by that trip to Marchmont."

"How right you are!" The car was threading its way through the traffic in the direction of Hampstead. "A few more coconuts shied at us would merely add to the jollity."

"Such as?"

"Alice Shane and Uncle Victor."

"Diarmid, you are worried! Why not chuck it for a time?"

"The last time I chucked it, I landed in the bog, saints and miracles and all. If I went with Codrill to Africa, ten to one Hector or some author would want a Moorish décor and the Sheikh would turn out to be Brierley junior or Uncle Victor. I wonder what did happen to Uncle Victor. I've often thought of putting an advert in *The Times*. 'Anyone able to offer information concerning Mr. Victor Naismith, bookmaker's clerk, of Victoria Road, St. John's Wood, London, please get in touch with Mr. Diarmid Riall, Charles Street, London, S.W.' Does anyone ever get an answer to that kind of thing?"

"I expect so. Was there a Brierley junior?"

"No. Not by Kirsty."

They were held up in the traffic at the approach to Fullers Gardens. As they sat there, a young Air Force pilot came to the edge of the pavement, glanced at them and the hold-up, and then proceeded to worm his way to the other side of the street. Lewis saw nothing extraordinary about him; he was musing on the possibility of the new Landon pleasing Sir Bruno; but beside him Diarmid was leaning forward, following the progress of the airman.

"Did you see him?"

"No. Who?" Lewis came back from his ruminations with a jerk.

"That young fellow."

"Air Force, wasn't he? Up on leave, I suppose."

"He had a definite look of Padraig about him."

"You're not going to tell me it was Sean O'Halloran, though it might well be, except you said he's in Australia. Or was it Hong Kong? It's not probable. More likely the Far East, in one of the trouble spots. All Irish look alike to me."

"It was the top part of the face, the

brow, the temples, the expression of the eyes. Longing . . ."

"What would he be longing for? Does he know he's Padraig's son?"

"He must know. They've lived in Dunphilly for years. His O'Halloran relations would have told him, whipped up his hatred of the man who allowed his mother to go."

"My dear chap, soon you'll be as bad as Padraig. Is this what happens when Kirsty writes to you? She'd better not repeat the performance. We'll have you in a nursing home . . ."

Diarmid's smile was bleak. "My apologies. A few weeks in Africa would be heaven after this damp fog."

They were at Roxhall Gardens. The car came to a halt before a house in the curving sweep of the Regency row and they descended and climbed the steps. Lewis pressed the bell button.

"Come in," said Russell Landon.

He was a tall, grey-haired gentleman with a world-wide reputation as a portrait painter. Diarmid thought he might have been anything from a barrister to a company director.

"Cigarette?"

They had been invited into a high, well-proportioned room overlooking the row. Diarmid's thoughts went a-chasing. Here, Kirsty had sat with Amos Brierley. "My housekeeper." It was a spacious room and he could imagine the two. In the artist's company she had taken on the poise and acquired the mentality to withstand that which came after.

"You know this house, Mr. Riall?"

"I do," he agreed. "While I was in Ireland, I met a Mrs. O'Halloran. She was employed by Amos Brierley who lived here before the war and from whom you purchased it."

"Ah!" Landon's thin, aristocratic face expressed interest. "Plumpish, matronly, motherly?"

"Not at all like Kirsty."

"I'm mistaken? The woman who was here after Amos was killed? The woman I talked to about the household details? She told me the tank in the roof would need replacing and the cistern in the lower lavatory was faulty. She showed me where a tile was off the studio roof. I was impressed by her soundness. The name was

O'Halloran. 'I'm Mrs. O'Halloran, Mr. Landon,' in a soughing, Irish voice. 'I've been authorised by Mr. Brierley's sister to help you in any way I can.' I wish she'd remained with me," he said.

"They were happy years" — Kirsty, telling him in the house in Dunphilly. "Amos was a kind employer." Aloud, he remarked: "She's been ill since then, seriously ill, with a disease that was said to be incurable but which vanished on a stormy night on Clunare. That's a holy island, near Marchmont, where I've been staying."

"I'll never understand you," said Landon. "I had a model once, from a place called of all names Ballycargy. Impossible! She came into a fair amount of money through a life assurance. You may have heard? It was in the papers. Now she's in Italy or France or somewhere on the Continent. Have you come across her, Hope?"

"I've seen portraits of her," replied Lewis, "only they were called by other names. The Marquesa de Nantis. The Countess of Wake. Madame Sesquierier."

"Yes. She had the most perfect figure. She carried her clothes as though they were made for her. There's one in the studio.

Dame Barbara Judd. She was the Red Cross Commandant. When they asked me for her portrait, she replied: 'I'm too short to make a good portrait, Russell. Can you do just head and shoulders?' The commission stated full length, in uniform. 'Don't worry,' I told her. 'I'll find a way,' but when I had finished it she would not let them have it; she said it wasn't her. Nobody else had complained of the perfect figure. Barbara Judd, however, was not the normal kind of woman. Not until she is dead will the Red Cross have her portrait. Meanwhile, it's there in the studio. You want to see the 'Arbour', Hope? I can't guess who would want it."

"Sir Bruno Waldstein."

"Oh, indeed!" His lips pursed. "It's not his usual choice."

"He wants an early Landon. Have you any others?"

"Unfortunately not. None that I'd care to sell to him." He led the way through the house to the garden. Much of it was as Kirsty had described it. Diarmid felt he had been there before.

"Does it matter if he wants them?" asked Lewis.

"You'll say I'm particular. I like to feel my work is worthy of the price."

"Not every painter is so concerned." Lewis went forward with an exclamation. "Is this it? I like it. Sir Bruno will like it. It has your hallmark, Russell, before you gained your reputation for portraits. They may be good, are good," glancing at the large canvas on his left. "I see what you mean. That head doesn't match the body. I saw Barbara at Peeping. My aunt is a great philanthropist; she knows her very well; she would say you have excelled yourself, beyond the realms of exactitude. This though is easier, softer, full of changing colours, a beautiful canvas. I'd no idea."

The painter's gaze was a trifle wistful. "It brings back moments of joy with a beloved person who would have none of me. Don't bother," as Lewis began his condolences. "I was cured long ago. But I've kept it in case. It's immaterial where it goes. She died last month, childless, without kin. Otherwise, I could have given it in memory. If Sir Bruno would like it, he can have it."

"He'll treasure it. It's exquisite, Russell."

"Inspired. I loved her deeply. It was her favourite spot where I could always find her. I was little more than a youth. What one does before experience touches one is more innocent and therefore more pure. Five hundred pounds, Hope."

"He'd give you double that."

"Should I double it? No, I won't barter my happiness. Too many fools do that and regret it afterwards. If it were you, now, I'd let it go — "

"A pity I spoke. I'll collect it tomorrow and you'll get your cheque within the week. He's a prompt payer."

"If I can be of any help," said Diarmid, "I'm going down to Winter's Grace."

"The conveyor of an inspiration," murmured Landon. "I envy you, Riall. What's caught your eye? Oh, that Brierley. I found it tucked away in a corner, obviously forgotten. It's not particularly good, a rough sketch of a harassed woman. He did them often, somebody told me — "

"The beloved?"

"My secret. It doesn't matter. She's dead. She was Brierley's sister. I met her when he and I attended an art course in Suffolk."

Diarmid's memory was racing madly. "Alice? Didn't she marry an Elliott Shane? She employed Kirsty O'Halloran before she came to Amos. In fact, she brought Kirsty. When Amos died, she got in touch with you and asked you if you'd buy the house?"

"Not quite. I saw the announcement and came to offer my sympathy. Good manners, Riall. She came to see the solicitors. She was by then nothing like the girl I had known. It was a bitter experience."

"You bought the house though?"

"I liked it. I remembered Amos as I had known him. He'd have some pungent things to say about Alice. I recollect he once said, when I was madly in love: 'You'd regret it, Russell. Much better let her go'."

"Kirsty said they were incompatible. She found her hard, grasping, an insatiable employer, too deep in good works. Kirsty was a sinner and not a particularly repentant one at that when Alice tried to rehabilitate her."

"Is she, this Kirsty O'Halloran, available?"

"She offers herself as a housekeeper for

periods of a few months. Amos left her enough to buy a house and furnish it comfortably. She has a portrait. You'd give your brows to get it, Lewis. As she must have been at the beginning of the war."

"You must ensure its survival for posterity, Diarmid."

"She'll never part with it. There's the memory of their relationship. Nothing immoral. She had touched the bottom — with my brother. It is a chain of coincidences. Put it in a book and nobody would believe it. Make it into a play and they'd say it was engineered. I'm trying to get Kirsty to come to the opening, to see her room, but she's learning the Latin, begod."

"Latin!" repeated Landon.

"Because of a certain Book of Cuimin which I found on a deserted island and which has since proved to be the finest book ever written in that part of Ireland."

"The Book of Cuimin. Good heavens, you don't tell me you and Kirsty are in that?"

"Indeed, we are, with Padraig and Marcia French and Alec Codrill. A long story, it is, and I've not the time to recount

it this afternoon but another time, when I'm
not up to my eyes. 'Tis more than grateful
I am for the pleasure you've given me and
would you mind keeping the Brierley for
me? I might need it anon, when the
workings of fate have made a few more
circumambulations."

2

HE drove smoothly and leisurely through the Surrey lanes. The feverish round of London was behind him, sloughed off like an unwanted skin; he was going to Marcia. He wanted badly to see Marcia. In the midst of turbulence, she was an island of solace. No doubt, when he reached her or rather Winter's Grace, he'd be caught up in the whirl of a houseparty, loaded with further commissions. He must be firm, knowing it needed only a second's irrelevance to set him off on some grandiose scheme.

He saw a sign to Childwell. Hadn't Marcia said it was near there, a mile, half a mile? He swung the wheel round and cruised easily, seeking the gates. Like everything about Jeremy, the engine was high-powered and tuned to a degree.

There was a pair of stone gate-posts, with gates wide open. A tweed-clad figure was coming down the drive.

"I thought it was time you were due."

She got in beside him. "Had a good journey?"

"She purrs like a cat. Your instructions were excellent," he told her. "How's the Professor? Will he be here?"

"No. He's making the final arrangements for Garraseesh. We sail in a fortnight."

"So soon!" aghast.

Lightly: "You sound affected."

"We'll do the Lord Mayor's Show."

"The tickets are in my room. Father's impressed by your work. He's going to enjoy himself."

"I'm glad." He drove along the drive to the house, a late Queen Anne residence of regal proportions. "The name's rewarding on a dull November day. It looks satisfying and graceful."

"Whereas Marchmont — ?"

"The west coast of Ireland is not exactly a Surrey hinterland. To each locality its architecture. Where do I put the car?"

"In the stables. Round there to the right."

There were only two other cars in the yard. Driving into the space she indicated, he asked her: "Am I early?"

"No. Just in time for tea."

"It's not a house-party?"

"Only the family," reassuring him. "It's Father's birthday. Anne-Louise is here too."

"Who's Anne-Louise?"

"Father's other adopted daughter."

"Oh!" he interrogated. "Does he make a habit of adopting daughters?"

"It's just taken place. This week, in fact. That's why you haven't heard about it. She was living with her father in China. A missionary," said Marcia.

"In these days?"

"They had moved to Hong Kong where he taught in a school. In August he died of cholera and one of his acquaintances wrote to Father. He immediately asked Anne-Louise here. She's a nice child."

He followed her to the front of the house. Inside, in the warm panelled hall a bright fire was burning. Several people were round the hearth. Marcia introduced him.

"Mummy, this is Diarmid. You've heard Father speak of him. He's doing the show next week."

Diarmid took Bernice Waldstein's hand

and liked the unwieldly motherly size of her. She might be Lady Waldstein and prospective Lady Mayoress but she was at heart the same untempered girl who had married Bruno when he was an ambitious dedicated youth starting in the insurance world of Lloyd's.

"Marcia has told me about you," she remarked.

Then Sir Bruno was enquiring: "How's everything, Riall? All sewn up?" He was a man of more than ample proportions, though not tall, with pebble, cutting eyes and a jutting nose. His hair was iron grey and his jowls dark. His hands as he held them over his growing corporation were chubby and well-manicured. His voice was that of a man ingrained with authority but tinged with humanity. In his country home he was cordial, indulgent and hospitable.

"It should all be ready, sir," Diarmid told him. "Chester's putting the finishing touches while I'm down here."

"Good man!"

Soon after, the knight left them to retreat to his study. "Send my tea in to me," he said to his wife. Even at the weekend, the wizard brain had to add to the compilations.

A young girl was coming shyly from the direction of the stairs. Seeing her, Marcia hurried forward.

"Anne-Louise, come and meet Diarmid." She took the young hand and urged her forward.

"How do you do?" said Diarmid. "You're finding life in England strange? So did I when I was ten, whipped away from Marchmont where Marcia's been digging," with a flash of droll humour at her, "and dropped into St. John's Wood like a pea from a pod. Begorra," he exclaimed, "the plainness and the dryness of that establishment. She was kind, my Aunt Ma-Ma, but she was not my mother. Uncle Victor was a bookmaker's clerk, nothing at all like my father who was a westerly wind chasing the sheep from the Pins. But I lived," he encouraged this fairy slip of a girl with the adorable name. "I buried myself in my drawings and set the house to rights in my own fashion."

"Diarmid's an interior decorator," explained Marcia. "He's designing the sets for Father's day on Saturday."

215

The forget-me-not blue eyes were losing their shyness; a faint nimbus light was shining in them, as his luring Irish burr tried to captivate her.

"What is it you've been doing in China, begod? A vast country, alanna. I'll be away to it one day when I've finished with ancient saints and Moorish palaces, and Marcia here and that antiquarian of an employer have decided to investigate the Cho-Ling dynasty of a thousand years ago."

"Don't lead her up the path," admonished Marcia.

Tea had arrived on a trolley and she moved to pour out. Anne-Louise lifted a plate of sandwiches and handed it to him.

"I am meaning it," said Diarmid. "The world is full of treasures to explore. Soon my clients will have exhausted the usual settings for their masques. An imported Chinese mandarin would be creating a stir. I must suggest it to Carrie Throssell. And you must help me, Anne-Louise. I work in Camden, in a narrow passage, in a converted warehouse. It's not unlike the back pathways of a foreign city, with a Chinese laundry within reach."

"Diarmid, I never saw a Chinese laundry. And Anne-Louise is not Chinese," laughing.

"Don't mind him," said Anne-Louise. "I've heard of the Irish blarney."

"Indeed you have, my sweeteen!" He shook his head at her and took his cup of tea from Marcia.

The Landon was on the wall in the drawing-room.

"I saw it last week, sir, before it was purchased. Lewis is a great friend of mine."

"I knew you thought up that Venetian palace for him." The knight was standing four square admiring his purchase. "Hope's excelled himself. I wanted the 'Summer Day' but this is better."

"Easier, freer, with more fluency than in his present pictures."

"I find it satisfying," stated Sir Bruno. "You're a fellow of discernment," taking a Monet cigar from an ivory box.

"May I be returning the compliment? I've heard sound things of you as a landlord."

"It's a small world, Riall. I knew I'd

approve of any fellow Marcia wished on me. When I saw you first, I sized you up as a willing, hard-working young chap, though the Irish was abhorrent. Slippery customers, the Irish."

"My mother was English, sir."

"So was mine, God bless her. A woman of gold, my mother, Riall, married to a genius. I don't know how she bore it. She brought up six children, myself and five sisters. There's only Rhoda and I left; and she's in America. Threw herself away on a scientific fellow. Lowther Cranch. That's his name."

"I was reading his paper in the *Globe*."

"You're not a scientist, Riall?" surprisedly. "I can't follow him at all. Obtuse, thick-skulled." He shook his head in wonder. "Came from Germany or Poland in '39. I can't see him getting a rocket to the stratosphere."

It was pure guesswork that Sir Bruno disliked his brother-in-law because he had taken his sister but doubtless correct. The Waldsteins had been a close-knit family and Rhoda's back-sliding in choosing an unrealistic scientist and another country — though Sir Bruno had connections with California and almost every city in the world — had left its mark. That and the tragedy of his own lack of children.

Diarmid learned from Marcia that there had been a boy, a brilliant child for whom all manner of successes had been foretold, but he had gone to the war, against his father's wishes, and been lost over London.

"Part of a plane fell on Father's office in Lombard Street and there were the markings CH-YZ on the wing. Solly's plane was CH-YZ."

They had gone to the terrace, after dinner. She had put on a thick camel coat over her velvet dress and he had flung on the astrakhan ulster in which he had travelled.

"My dear," he was unaware of the deeper mode of address, "how very tragic!"

"Father took it hardly. He had made plans for Solly to go into the business. Had there not been the war he would have been an executive of Waldstein's by now, carrying on the tradition in the City. It wouldn't have mattered so much if he hadn't been accepted by all as Father's successor, if he hadn't known and wanted to do it, if he hadn't spent his youth preparing himself, in his spare time going to Waldstein's and making himself familiar with the business."

"How old was he?"

"Seventeen. He told the authorities he was nineteen. Being a Jew he looked older. He was already losing his hair; he used to joke about it and say he was no advertisement for Colcreem. He had learned to fly unbeknown to Father, with a friend from the Green Coat School, a man who is now a pilot on the Trans-African Airways. Capt. Brent said he was brilliant. He was not surprised when Solly volunteered and was accepted; or when he was given a Hurricane and began to collect 'scalps' as soon as the Battle of Britain was on. There were eleven marks on the fuselage which fell in the street."

"And he?"

"They never found his body. They presumed he fell in the Thames. He couldn't swim That surprises you? None of the Waldsteins can swim. It's a failing, come down in their ancestry. Nobody can prove it would have saved him but the hope cannot be completely ignored."

"It's doubtful," he replied. He had watched the combats when he was a boy, the silver trails weaving and diving and spinning and twisting like agitated eels in the enamelled sky, and Uncle Victor coming in with the latest edition. "Eighty-nine today, Diarmid. We've got 'em licked." At the price of boys like Solly Waldstein and his kind, leaving their fates and giving their lives for their country.

"The only memorial is a piece of a Hurricane fighter with CH-YZ marks in a room at Waldstein House, the room which would have been Solly's had he lived."

"What happens to Waldstein's?"

"Only Father knows. The other directors haven't been told. They've asked, to be presented with his 'blank' face. All the expression goes from his features and his eyes harden like stone; you have the impression that the man in the outer clothes is dead. I've seen it." She shivered. "I never want to see it again."

Involuntarily, he put his arm round her shoulder. "In Ireland," he whispered, "you told me he was generous."

"He is, but he's also grasping. If Anne-

Louise doesn't mind, she'll be sucked into his orbit."

"She looks at the moment as though she would not mind very much."

"It would be bad for her," instantly. "She must fight. She must find a job."

"Poor Anne-Louise. I feel sorry for her. Why not take her to Africa with you?"

"Father would refuse."

"He has plans, I am sure."

"You must remember Anne-Louise only came six days ago. And first we must see him installed as Lord Mayor. He's working on his speech. It has to be better than anybody else's. I'm very fond of Father," she averred, "but I can see he has faults. He's dazzled by his eminence."

"All great men are. Are you warm enough?"

"Tiring of our stolen hour?"

"Marcia!"

She leaned a little closer. "I like to tease you, Diarmid. When we come back from Garraseesh . . ."

"I'm dreading the parting."

"You'll be busy."

"Alanna," he breathed, "there is a heart beating in my breast."

In the dusky light, he could just see her face, finely-moulded, full of character, that had gained stature from her insistence on full independence.

"Diarmid, you child!" She held out her hand and caught his fingers and squeezed them. "Come inside. We're getting cold and we don't want to sneeze at the Lord Mayor's Banquet; and," she spoke shyly, "there's tomorrow. When the sun shines in wintertime at Winter's Grace you see why the house was given its name."

Banks of trees in their autumn clothing. Russet and gold and burning red and a few deep green and amber and henna. The artist in Diarmid leaped at the contrasts, storing the vista and envisaging it reproduced in halls and on stages. Walking with him that Sunday morning, her low-heeled shoes battening down the fallen leaves, Marcia saw a man she had barely glimpsed and had to cling hard to her self-imposed control. There was Algeria in a fortnight and absence from this laughing, madly-tantalising, wildly attractive Irishman who was doing odd and indescribable things to her being. She had promised the Professor . . . and she had a contract; she liked the work; she would be unhappy away from it; she had fought for her right to do it, and to capitulate now . . .

"Penny!" said Diarmid.

"You were far away," she retorted.

"Only as far as those trees. What are they?"

"Chestnut. Beech. Sycamore. Oak. Whichever way you look they're all around."

"Protecting you," he stated. The thought was warm and particular. He would have preferred her here permanently, encaged in this rampart of gold.

"You want to see them in spring when the buds are breaking."

"I refuse to consider them finer than they are now. It is Winter's Grace, after all." The name hung like a poem on his tongue as he infused it with meaning. "The grace of God's bounty. In a place like this, Marcia, one can feel the holy touch."

Not in wild rocky islands? But she had no wish to upbraid him. The touch of more than loveliness was on her heart, in her sight and touch and sense. Would her father and mother agree? He was nothing in the City . . . but, glowing, with verve, fighting for her option, he was something in the circles that attracted attention. Diarmid Riall, interior decorator, producer of backcloths so tremendous . . . She laughed. Her caprices held her tightly, prompting her steps to a sylphic lightness. He had a warehouse. Sir Bruno had several warehouses. "St. Cuimin never came here."

He refused to be diverted. "Other saints trod these ways. You of all people must agree to that. On a morning like this you can picture them, tramping to Canterbury. Marcia, let's follow them, put our packs on our backs and turn our faces to the sun and seek . . . what shall we seek?"

"Our own holy spot."

He was standing in front of her, bestride the path.

"Do you mean that?" wonderingly.

She was silenced. Whatever the turmoil in her breast, she had no intention as yet, before she had fulfilled her role . . . She had not meant to speak as she had. He had tricked her into it, with his bemusing chatter. As Padraig had tricked Kirsty . . . Was she defending the 'lovely woman'?

"Wouldn't we seek a holy spot if we were pilgrims?" uncertainly. Be firm, Marcia French. Hold on to your resolve. Withstand this invader who has come into your country. "You're intelligent enough — "

He was laughing delightedly, tenderly, with a knowledge in his gaze. "Marcia!" he said, shaking his head at her. "Who's bewitched now? Who's fallen for the rites? Trees and the fabulous golden beauty of them, God's magnificent touch. There's a shine on your face, my dear that nobody but God could have put there. You've seen a glory — " He was holding her with both hands, bending closer.

"It's time we were going — "

"To our holy place? Isn't this our holy place? Our Winter's Grace? Marcia, my darling — " His arms were around her. "You can't fight the glory. You can't fight this thing that has come to us. You can't say: 'Diarmid Riall, I don't love you,' because I can see it, in your dear darling eyes, on your quivering lips, in every breathing part of you. It's not one scrap of use saying: 'Go away' to me, darling; 'I'm not having you,' because you've got me, now and every moment, in these private woods that were made for a morning like this."

"Diarmid! Oh dear — "

"There you are." He was jubilant; he kissed her. "You've taken the plunge. Is it cold you are, darling," gathering her close, "as cold as the frost on the winter bough or the seas pounding the rocks beyond the Reek? Or is it warmed by the glow of a heart's love, like the glimpse of a star in the black of the night? Uncle Victor said I had the lulling voice. I'd talk the devil from his hindmost. You should have known Uncle Victor. He was an unprohibitive companion; and a wizard with figures."

"We could do with him now, Diarmid, when we go to see Father — "

"Begod! I'd forgotten." He groaned; then he brightened. "You're over age. You're not Anne-Louise, eighteen and a bit. Who is Sir Bruno Waldstein to stand in our way? If he refuses, I'll not do his Lord Mayor's Show for him. How's that, darling? Bribery and corruption? Sir Bruno Waldstein held to ransom? Hector can refuse to pay his rent. He'll be on our side. You must meet Hector."

"I shall meet him on the first night; and, Diarmid, you're wasting your breath. We must hurry. It's twelve o'clock."

"Do you love me, Marcia?"

"I'm afraid so."

"Enough to marry me?"

"One day."

"Damn Codrill," he swore. "I suppose I lose you the moment the Show's over."

"You could pay us a visit at Garraseesh," wickedly. "You're forever talking about a Moorish palace. I'll look up the guide books and find the nearest one to the dig. Then you can browse all day long."

"If I come to Garraseesh it won't be to leave you to Codrill's sweet care."

She laughed, a soft, deep, loving and satisfied laugh that welled up into her throat and rose, sparkling and effervescent, to her eyes.

"Diarmid, I do love you."

"It's very honoured I am," he replied, "to be aware of it, Miss French." Then he kissed her again before they went running, hand in hand, along the leaf-strewn path beneath the trunks towering on either side resembling a cathedral of

nature to the house that was named,
magnanimously and miraculously Winter's
Grace.

3

THE Lord Mayor was giving his speech in Guildhall to the gathering that each year on this day assembled in that traditional place to do honour to the one chosen to represent the City and to toast the bastion that for nine hundred years had stood four square against every odd.

Marcia and Diarmid were far away from the top table but from their distant point they could see Sir Bruno, portly, distinctive, the ornate chain of office about his neck, the hundreds of brilliant lights glinting on his horn-rimmed spectacles and the bald patch on the top of his head as he unfolded the sheets of paper over which he had expended so much toil and thought and mind and sweat during the weeks that were past.

"I am deeply conscious of the honour which you have accorded me this day. It has long been my hope and my dream that I should one day stand here before you and address you as the representative of the oldest community of traders in the western hemisphere."

Cheers.

"He's enjoying himself, the dear," whispered Marcia. She was looking cool and desirable in a brocade evening gown, the colour of the woods at Winter's Grace. "My dear, the colour this year is amber. It's in all the shops. Don't you use your eyes?" He refused to be gainsaid. "It's our colour," he reiterated. "Thank you for wearing it." The past week had been epileptic with crises. The final preparations for the Show, Chester grumpy and testy, as always on the eve of an event, Jeremy recovered from his flu intent on driving Hector and Diarmid and all his cast to distraction, the secret of their love, delightful, precious, still only half realised, Codrill chattering about Garraseesh, Sir Bruno arriving at the warehouse unannounced and prowling like a beast after prey, asking innumerable questions, the decision to defer the announcement until after the Show when he would be more mellow and they hoped more amenable, the Lord Mayor installed at Guildhall . . .

"Pray for us, Marcia."

She gave him a glittering glance. "You did very well. He's delighted with the procession. He'll listen like a lamb."

"When do I come?"

"I'll tell you," she said. "I'll have to choose the moment."

"I may not be in."

"You must be in."

"Jeremy or Hector — "

"Diarmid, do you love me?"

"Alanna, don't tease me beyond bearing."

She caught his hand beneath the table. At the other end of the vast, glittering concourse, Sir Bruno was getting into his stride.

"I have taken as my theme this year the importance of the City in finance and trade in relation to the rest of the world. You all saw the procession this morning, created incidentally by a member of a 'foreign' nation who finds the atmosphere of London to his liking and benefit, who gleans his inspiration in a multitude of alleys. I shall not waste your time or mine in a recounting of what I think of that certain person . . . ."

Polite laughter.

"Oh Lord!" groaned Diarmid.

"Smile," prompted Marcia. "It's praise. It'll bring commissions to you. He can make or mar you — "

"I'll not be wanting to be made or marred. I'm doing very well, thank you," he said.

"Are you refusing me, Diarmid?"

"I'm for marrying you indeed, not the Lord Mayor of London."

She crinkled her lips. "When Father adopted me, he little knew what he was taking on."

"For nearly a century I and my forbears have been taking an active part in the financial life of this city . . ." Sir Bruno was continuing. The Lord Mayor's Banquet was proceeding according to tradition.

"You mean, young man," Sir Bruno said, sitting secure and solid behind his great desk in his study at the Mansion House, around him the appliances and appurtenances of wealth and position, "that you are asking me for the hand of my daughter Marcia." He was pompous and pedantic, indulging in the role of heavy parent, albeit by adoption. "I was not aware that she was in any way considering a change from her present status. She told me last night that she is going to Algeria, to Garraseesh, with Alec Codrill in two days' time."

"That's just it, sir," said Diarmid hurriedly. He had arrived to be taken on a tour of the Mansion House and Marcia had said: "Why not take your account into him? He's in a generous mood."

"I can't say I am entirely in agreement with this junketing round and as for un-earthing odd bits and pieces . . ."

"I'm entirely in agreement with you, sir." Diarmid discarded the memory of the excitement at Marchmont when the first portion of the list had been displayed. "That's the reason I am asking you. Marcia and I — "

"It appears," went on Sir Bruno in his most pompous and professional manner, "that while I have been imagining her working for that quaint and seductive fellow she was in actual fact turning her attention to more flippant matters."

"Not at all, sir," said Diarmid. He had

discerned a faint glitter in the knight's pearly eye. "She applied herself most studiously to the dig."

"Amazing," remarked Sir Bruno. "What these people find in the places is beyond me."

"In particular, it was an ancient chronicle. Professor Codrill has given it to the University of Dublin, to rest alongside other unique treasures."

"I can see nothing gainful in going back to the Middle Ages."

"Beyond," put in Diarmid. "St. Cuimin lived on Clunare from 520 to 561."

"Who?"

"St. Cuimin. It was St. Cuimin's Abbey they were seeking, as apart from his church."

"What, may I ask, will be the result when they are finished?"

"The same as it was in Corfu and the City . . ."

"You're surely not identifying the *City* with these troglodytes?"

"The Temple of Mithros, sir. You can't have forgotten. Mosaics and temple ornaments. The complete base of the building, revealed by the bombing. Your duty while you are Lord Mayor surely is to preserve the ancient sites and codes of this square mile . . ." He met the militant stare of his host. "On the past is built the future. You outlined it the other evening, mentioning the association of Waldsteins with the City of London and your fervent hope . . ."

"You're not a financier, young man."

"Unfortunately not, sir. The head for such calculations was not given me. If you had had the training of my brother when he was ripe for development, you might have had a Riall. But it's not a financier that appeals to me. I want to marry Marcia."

"If you can keep her from this absurd habit of going off with fellows like Codrill, you'll earn my gratitude. There's no earthly reason for her to do it."

"In her mind, Sir Bruno, there is. She's like you in one respect. She treasures her independence."

"Why can't she rest at home? Here I am, in the Mansion House, in the most coveted place in England, and she tells me she's going to Algeria. It's warmer there, she says, away from the fog and the damp. Mr. Riall, I love London; I love its pavements and buildings; I see in its continuance a further proof of its importance."

"Can I marry her, sir?"

"If you keep her from rushing off to the outposts of the world. Why, in Algeria, she might fall for a sheikh," slyly. "How are you going to ensure that doesn't happen?"

Diarmid relaxed. He saw he had won. The knight was not going to refuse him Marcia, though he was not over-enamoured of the thought of his prospective son-in-law. "Riall," he could hear him say to his contemporaries in the comfort of his club, "that fellow who designs things. Irish and looks it. Hasn't the first inclination to understand figures, unless it's the cheques he's receiving for those amazing creations. The modern world eludes me. Went to St. Withburga's and hangs out in a converted warehouse in Camden. Must say, though, he's got it well fitted up. Clever fellow in his way. Women fall for the most unexpected fellows. Went to Ireland with Codrill. He was there, trying to find a book or a church. Saints seem two a penny. Can't say I've had much to do with saints." Diarmid's lips curved into a happy smile.

"I'm going to Algeria too, sir," he said.

It was the first night of *The Irish Room*. When Hector was too indisposed to attend, a special television set was installed in his room and he watched the performance from his couch. It cost a fabulous fortune but Hector was rich, and the only person who objected was Sir Bruno who said the chimney stack was not stout enough to support the aerial. Nevertheless, the aerial was there; the television was tuned in; and Hector lay on his couch awaiting the presentation of his latest concoction to the critical audience of a first night.

Diarmid, who had called to see him on his way to collect Marcia, said brightly: "I've a mind to stay with you and see it from here. It might be more soothing on the nerves."

Hector smiled wanly. "I'm glad it has finally come. *The Room*'s given me white hairs. Jeremy's interpretation of the situation was, to say the least of it, bizarre. You had it better though why a room in Dunphilly when it takes place in Dublin . . ." He shook his head.

"All Irish towns are exactly alike," replied Diarmid. "The English say so and it's an English audience who'll be seeing it tonight. When it travels to Ireland, as it will, we'll have another décor."

"Your confounded house at the Royal, I suppose."

The twinkle in Diarmid's eye was appreciative. Hector's tone was pettish, the result of overstretched nerves and acute disappointment at missing the triumph.

"Your characters would be out of their element at the Royal."

"From all accounts," Burne riposted, "the present occupants are also."

Marcia jumped into the taxi he had secured and with a wide sweep they were heading back towards theatreland. She nestled against him. "Anne-Louise is jealous."

"We'll find her a nice young man whom Papa Lord Mayor will approve. Preferably one who is a wizard with figures."

"Not a pilot — "

"Are your parents following?"

"In the official car."

—He left her at the entrance to the box. "Jeremy must be told, and the management, and the cast." He vanished into the back portions of the theatre.

She was hardly seated when Sir Bruno and Lady Waldstein arrived. Anne-Louise slipped into the seat beside hers.

"You're going to enjoy this."

Diarmid came into the box. "Good-evening, sir. Good-evening, Lady Waldstein. Hallo, Anne-Louise."

"Anne-Louise wants to go back-stage," said Marcia.

"Her wish shall be granted. I shall be honoured to escort the two daughters of the Lord Mayor of London." He demanded: "Is it really I, Diarmid Riall, sitting in a box at the Circle in the company of my amber girl and Forget-me-not Blue and prosperous Sir Bruno and his wife? I shall wake up in an hour and be in my bed at my flat, cursing the telephone . . ."

"We're all feeling rather like that, Diarmid."

The crash of the orchestra brought

them to their feet for the National Anthem and then the curtain rose and they strained forward to see Hector Burne's latest drama.

"Remarkably effective." Sir Bruno turned to Diarmid after the first act. "I normally think theatre settings rather amateurish, stagey if you will forgive the remark, but this room of yours . . ."

"It really exists, sir, in Dunphilly." He could feel Marcia listening carefully while Anne-Louise was over-excited and pink-flushed. "It is in fact the sitting-room of my brother's wife. I was studying the play while I was in Ireland and it appealed to me as the setting for the events Hector had advised."

"I congratulate you," said Sir Bruno. He was still in his mind with the players. "That portrait on the wall behind the door. Odd place to hang it. Is it real?"

"It is a portrait of my sister-in-law by Amos Brierley. She was his housekeeper for many years after she parted from my brother."

"Brierley, eh? I'd like another of his. Would she sell?"

"I'm sure she would not."

241

"Offer her a thousand pounds," promptly.

"Bruno," said Bernice, "you haven't seen it."

"This fellow has. And Brierley never did anything slipshod. Will you be seeing her?"

"In the spring when the dig re-opens, unless Padraig sends for me sooner. He's affected with strange ideas."

"He's not the only one," said Sir Bruno. "There's many in the City. Have you put Eric Frost on to him?"

"Sir Eric saw him in December."

"Then you needn't worry. Eric's the best man in the country." Sir Bruno sat back in his seat. "Next interval, dear," as the curtain began to rise.

So now he had an offer of a thousand pounds to convey to Kirsty, for a portrait she valued beyond price . . . and Sir Bruno beaming with accomplishment! "I invariably succeed" — a remark at Winter's Grace, in the warmth and companionship of his family. "There is little to which I turn my hand . . ." — the Lord Mayor's Banquet. Mother of God, hear me, he prayed. Keep a little of your compassion for me. If he takes a dislike to me, I may lose my Marcia. He turned quickly and met her gaze.

"Come outside. Poor dear! You have landed yourself in a spot. What made you include that portrait in the set?"

"St. Cuimin, or the fates," wryly. He pushed his hand through his dark, thick hair. "I shall have to make myself uncomfortable with Kirsty. She'll be furious. She regards Amos as sacrosanct."

"So much for the lovely woman," slyly.

"She'll have to sell," he persisted. "I shall tell her my life depends on it, that her need of the portrait is nothing compared to mine for you."

"Are you gambling my love for a pottage of money?"

"Be silent!"

"You're upset. It was bound to happen," she remarked. "Father usually manages to gain the whip hand."

"You told me he was generous."

"Isn't a thousand pounds generous for a picture he hasn't seen? Personally, I'd call it stupid."

" 'Tis the most beautiful thing you ever saw. Pst! Wait! There's one in

Landon's studio, an earlier one, of Kirsty as she was when she arrived in London with Alice Shane. She doesn't know of it. I little thought, when I saw it with Lewis, I'd need it so soon. Tomorrow I'll get it."

"Tomorrow will be too soon. You couldn't have been to Ireland and back in so few hours."

"The childishness of me!" He ruefully acknowledged her sense. "You'll be good for me, my darling. Nevertheless, I'll collect it and take it to Sir Bruno in a week, before I follow to Algeria."

"I shall have to wait until March to see it."

"You will go to Algeria," he retorted. "You will miss all the events in the court circular."

He blew a kiss at her.

4

THE hot dry wind had more than sun in it. It had sand and grit and glare and whirled around his legs as he stepped from the truck that had brought him to Garraseesh. But the sight of a cool-clothed figure coming towards him quickly over the sand, her hand outstretched, banished the discomfort and the heat.

"Diarmid, at last."

He took her in his arms. "A time I've had," he confessed, looking to see if she were the same. "You'll never guess. I'm run off my feet. You look wonderful!"

"It's not very successful. Use your charm on the Professor. He's low."

"No Moorish castle?" He raised his brows.

"No help from the Sheikh. Obstruction all the way. I wouldn't be surprised if he packed up. It's not what he's used to."

"I wouldn't be dissuading him, my darling, though now I am here I'd like to see Algeria."

"What kept you so long?"

"Hector's Pratt."

"Oh. Ill?"

"He's got peritonitis," he said.

"That's serious."

"Very," he agreed. He was taking in the dig. The hills in the background, the palms. Wonderful for a scene for Effie Clanrobin's Moorish Ball. In a trice, his pencil and notebook were busy. "Just a moment," he said. "It's what I've been wanting. Effie rang me last week. She'd heard I was coming to Garraseesh. Would I do an Eastern ball? I said quite firmly Garraseesh was in Algeria. Wasn't that the East, she enquired. Anyway, wherever it was, she wanted it. She's a poppet but a dumb poppet. I said I would. Hence my delight when Garraseesh fits the requirements."

"She'd probably swotted it beforehand," prosaically. "The Clanrobins aren't clueless. Hector's left without Pratt?"

He nodded. "That was more serious. He rang me in a dither. Did I know of anybody who would come while Pratt was in hospital? The agencies were useless; his was a special case; he had to have the best; after all, Pratt had been with him for

246

years; and he was starting a new play —
The Sycamore Square — did I remember?
I'd given him the idea for it. So it was up
to me, if I didn't want his masterpiece
ruined — "

"Really," said Marcia, "you're like
children, the pair of you. Whom did you
find?"

"Guess?" His eyes sparkled in his glee.
"You won't be approving. Hector does.
He's as pleased as punch. Purring like a
cat. Says he's never been better looked
after and he's not sure he won't pension
off Pratt."

"Diarmid, don't prattle so!"

"The last person you'd think of and the
last person you'd expect, but the only one,
I knew with experience, who took jobs at
short notice and for an unspecified time.
Fortunately, I'd got the picture from
Landon."

"Diarmid" — the import of his words
began to penetrate — "you're not telling
me Hector's new help is Kirsty O'Halloran?"

"Indeed I am." He shut the notebook.
"Isn't that a miracle for you? Now show
me the dig," before she had time to com-

ment. "Give me the history so I can talk to the Sheikh when I meet him."

"He's a highly arrogant young man. The French found him impossible and now Algeria is independent — "

"He's in the Government. I know. Make enough song and dance and you get what you want. Your father's very well, by the way, and Anne-Louise has found herself a beau." On his face was a sportive, unreadable expression.

"Now what?"

"I'm afraid you're going to say the Irish are impossible as well as Algerian sheikhs."

"Tell me," she commanded.

They had almost reached the dig. In the dip of the land the team could be seen dispersed over the area. The Professor was bending over an excavation, a panama hat on his head, a white handkerchief fluttering from the base of it over his skinny neck.

"I took Anne-Louise to see Hector. You remember I promised she should meet the author of *The Irish Room*. She was thrilled, literally jumping up and down with excitement. I've never seen her so intense. She looked beautiful, with a sheen on her

248

cheeks and her eyes glittering like stars. Anybody would fall in love with her. I nearly did myself. The old chap was delighted. He can be pleasing when he chooses and this unguarded innocence touched his cynical heart and took him back to the days of his youth. He was telling her when he had started, in a back room in Holborn, scribbling half-way through the night, then trudging the pavements in search of a producer, climbing rickety stairs in narrow buildings, and Kirsty was there too, listening with that keenly receptive air that makes you wonder why Padraig persists in his bigotry, and the street bell rang. 'I'll answer it,' says Kirsty. Out she goes and Hector carries on with his tale, until suddenly he says: 'Where's Kirsty? She's been gone a long time. I'd like my fillip. Anne-Louise must want some refreshment too. See if you can find her, there's a good fellow.' I had been hearing low voices in the hall, soft, slurring Irish voices, and I think I was not unprepared for what I found."

"The boy?"

He replied: "It was Sean, home on leave and posted to Chipping Upton. He'd been to Dunphilly and found his mother flown.

Father O'Rourke had given him her address and he'd come to tell her he was there. And, Marcia," his voice took on a sterner note, "he was that boy I saw, in Fullers Gardens, crossing the traffic block, as like to his father as he himself must have been when he left Uncle Patrick's. Hard! He whipped out at me and said why had I used his mother's sitting-room for my set; he'd been to the theatre and seen it; hadn't I any shame? From him, the son of Padraig! I had a meeting with that young man and a great many things were said. He has the unyielding Riall pride and he says Marchmont should be his when Padraig is gone, as it should, begorra, only his name is O'Halloran, without we change it by deed poll, but that Kirsty refused. They're a fine pair, I must say. Hector can sort that one out for the moment."

"You said Anne-Louise — ?"

"We had to go into the study. Hector rang his bell and Anne-Louise came out to see where we were and those two took one look at each other and — I'm sorry, my darling. When the god of love touches two young things — "

"You can't be serious!" she said.

"She's never had a boy before," softly. "He's never seen anyone so lovely as Anne-Louise. Let them be, Marcia. There'll be tears enough when your father is told."

"I must write to her," thickly. "She can't, so soon after coming to us — " Helplessly, she appealed to him.

"The beauty of it," he sighed. "Innocent, wondering, like the opening of a rose bud. You wouldn't believe it, Marcia alanna . . ."

"I can imagine Father's reaction. Good heavens, Diarmid, a wild Irish pilot . . ."

"Would it have been better if I had not stolen you?" he enquired. "I've apologised to Sean for that. He's a clever young man. He'll have an eye to the main chance. The Air Force has nearly lost its claim. It's foreseeing him, I am, in an office in the City, computing figures."

"What are you saying now? Are you crazy?"

"Last night," he went on, "Sean O'Halloran visited Sir Bruno with a view to seeking employment in Waldstein's Bank. I gave him a testimonial and so did Hector. The one from his commanding officer spoke of his integrity and intelligence."

Bleakly: "He's a pilot — "

"Don't worry, Marcia. He knows about Solly. It sobered him and calmed him in no time. He once lost a pal, in an accident. He's acquainted with frustration and loss."

"Does that mean," in a strangled voice, "the 'lovely woman' is going to be connected by marriage with the Waldsteins?"

"She already was, by my loving you, but she won't intrude," said Diarmid. "She has the manners, that woman. When Hector's Pratt is well, she'll go back to Dunphilly and keep herself to herself."

"Until you ferret her out for another of your friends," chokingly.

"Darling, I couldn't think of anyone else, and Hector was desperate."

He spent two happy days at the dig, endeavouring to rally Alec Codrill who was convinced that Sheikh Abou-el-Tourin was hindering him in all he wanted to do. He also dined with Abou-el-Tourin and found him, as Marcia had said, arrogant, ambitious and intolerant of odd, skinny Englishmen who bent over holes in the sand.

"Has he nothing better to do?" in a

cultivated Oxford accent, his French impeccable as well as his English.

"He loves it," said Diarmid. He was sitting cross-legged on the floor of the guest-chamber. Before him Abou-el-Tourin sat likewise but more at ease in the unusual pose. It made the thighs ache. He would be less stiff after a ramble on the Reek or a walk through the woods at Winter's Grace. "He is one of those men who reside in the past."

"I live in the future," said Abou-el-Tourin.

"Most of us do. It's force of circumstances, though we draw our inspiration from the past. In Algeria," carefully, aware of the recent years of strife and killing before the French surrendered, "you are attempting to build a fresh civilisation based on your natural environment and ideals. It is taking all your energies and the energies of your countrymen. Bitterness and turmoil have to be erased; trust and integrity replaced. Where you stand now, we stood in '22. The scars are still painful and visible."

Abou-el-Tourin leaned forward. His lean tanned face, more like a hawk's than any Diarmid had previously seen, took on a look of avarice. "You are a son of an injured race! You would not be like that ungrateful infidel my father engaged and for whom I have so much hatred — "

Wild tales of the Foreign Legion began to dance in Diarmid's mind, read on the carpet in Victoria Road . . .

"The Englishman, Victor Naismith."

"Victor — " Diarmid gasped as in a nightmare. "In Garraseesh!" It could hardly be. Victor Naismith, the husband of Aunt Ma-Ma, had been a bookmaker's clerk, a puny little man who went regularly to his office and returned each evening with the "pink 'un". He occasionally passed on a "dead cert" which Diarmid mislaid until the horse won and Victor said he should have put his "shirt on" but Aunt Ma-Ma was particular about his shirts; he put too much paint and crayon on them, lying on his stomach on the floor.

"He came with a foolproof system for raising money," said the Sheikh. "He was very wealthy."

Victor's wild fling, begorra! Diarmid's thoughts were careening like tribesmen in the desert.

254

"His tongue was like honey. He would instruct my father in exchange for a suite of apartments in the palace and a title, the overseer of the treasury. At that time the fortunes of my family were low. The French had appropriated all but the barest needs. My father had his title but little money, his palace but few retainers; he was beholden to the French for his mode of existence. It was after Sidi Adalini," bitterly.

Desperately grasping at his reeling senses, Diarmid guessed that Sidi Adalini had been a trouble spot in the desert, an ambush, an annihilation.

"In many ways my father was a simple man. A good man," said Abou-el-Tourin who evidently was not, in the same sense, 'a religious man'. "He accepted the man from Tangier and made him his Treasurer."

Around him the silks and hangings danced a mocking gyrotome. The archways and columns of the chamber advanced towards him in lurid pantomime. It was the wine, innocently golden, wickedly potent.

"He wore the Moorish robes and the

255

fez. It gave him poise, for he was a tiny man."

Four feet seven, thought Diarmid, going back to a day in the Victoria Road when Victor had taken him into a chemist's shop and they had weighed themselves, soberly and in commutation, and been measured. "Next time you'll have caught me up, you rascally Riall."

"He lived in state, as befitted an official in the employ of Sheikh Abdul-el-Tourin, and for a time our fortunes improved. We made money in a variety of ways, thanks to the adroitness of his tricks, and I was able to go to Oxford and imbibe the learning of the English and to Paris where I learned to understand the mentality of our oppressors. For that I am grateful." The emotionless tone grated on the sweetness of the proffered fruits, dates and figs. "I returned to find my father almost bankrupt, the fortunes squandered, the French in tighter control, Victor-el-Tangier in disgrace. He had made a blunder, a glaring mistake, and the French Commissioner, a cleverer man than the infidel, had 'smelt a rat', you say?" The bizarre enquiry was like a cockatoo in a gathering of swans. Uncle Victor had always succumbed to Aunt Ma-Ma's more reasonable logic. "He unearthed machinations of such proportions that even my father was staggered. He was then almost blind, the result of wounds in the desert, and completely in the hand of his official. If the infidel said: 'Give me the shekels,' he gave them. He surrendered his keys; he made his treasures available to the upstart; he was betrayed. I went in to see him, after the Commissioner had summoned me to his room — in *this* palace," sharply, "I, the Sheikh Abou-el-Tourin, educated at Oxford and the Sorbonne, summoned like a schoolboy, to hear the hated foreign voice telling me . . . He was a traitor. He had sold us, hook, line and sinker, to our deadliest enemy. He had gambled our fortunes, amassed by my father in his raids on the oases, and the 'kitty' was bare. We owed our existence and the future of our name to Monsieur Commissioner le Cocque who informed me concisely that we were valuable to the French if we would obey his instructions and engage in no open combat and live in muted splendour. We, the Sheikhs of Tourin, renowned as warriors and leaders! I, Abou-el-Tourin, to lounge about my palace, a useless peony! Because of the treachery of an English infidel. I went to my father. I demanded he be surrendered to me. I would deal with him. As I have said, my father was a good man, a blind man, but still, he informed me, the Sheikh of Garraseesh. While he lived, he would have no usurping of his authority. He would know if I made any move to thwart his rule. I knew his threat. I knew his sharp ears, his hand on his knife. He would not hesitate to remove me if necessary and substitute my brother Majed-el-Tourin in my stead. A man does not need to see his enemy. I must go warily, I must bide my time with the infidel, steel myself to confront him in his Moorish robes, his silly face a-grin from his escape, uncondemned by that old man; but I would act when I was Sheikh."

Diarmid shuddered. As the harsh, fierce voice flowed on, the tall lean arrogant figure sat upright on the cushion with the taut awareness of the hawk hovering over its prey, and he tried to fathom the incredible position, but beyond the fact that it had begun in Tangier, he could reach no acceptable conclusion. Against his will he was bound to listen to the extended tale of lust and treachery, the battle of two Moors, father and son, for the supremacy of a fabulous palace and a strip of territory. It was like a story in *The Boys Own Paper*, bought by Aunt Ma-Ma once a week with her *Sunday Companion* and *Home Notes*. For the space of one moment, the pieces fell into their relevant places. Uncle Victor, the downtrodden, the ordinary, the bookmaker's clerk, perusing the *Paper*, reading out odd paragraphs to Diarmid. "That's the life, lad. A Moorish castle. A Pelopennesian island." He could hear it faintly through the mists of memory, high-toned and squeaky, getting out of control, the undersized body fidgeting in the hard chair. "When we make our fortunes, we'll go, shall we, and live with the princess?" Everybody's fairy tale, the everlasting unattained dream of ordinary man, no more and no less than millions of others, in parlours and front rooms, over the tea cups or the dahlias, imagining vast vistas and soaring realms. He had dreamed his own dreams . . . and found a disused warehouse in which to house them.

"He was inventing a new plan. It was to

restore the lost shekels and increase them to millions. He went to Tangier, to Morocco, Brindisi. The man had courage of a kind," allowed Abou-el-Tourin, "driven by the knowledge that I would have his throat the moment my father gave up the grip. He was working against time. Though he said nothing and would deprive the infidel of nothing, saying the dog was easier to manage with his bone, he had been disturbed by the disaster; he had lost faith in the wizardry of the man from Tangier; he had little hope of seeing the plan come to fruition. Yet like a blind man clutching a straw he clung to the hope. His eyes were fast going; the glare of the desert was too much for them so he remained in his palace and delegated his duties to his sons; I, he made head justicar and commandant of his army; I had the freedom of his territory and the right to kill; but I must not take the Treasurer. The ingratiating voice still had power to make my father feel the great man he had been. Despite his witchery with figures, he knew little about the sheikhdom, the actual conditions of tribesman and economy; he had — what do they say? — a one-track mind. By juggling figures he could present to himself and to my father a dazzling prospect of riches. And my father, rapidly being barred from active participation, grasped the reed offered by the wheedling jackal and kept his favourite by him."

The silk-robed figure stirred on the piled cushions. In the movement of the limbs was lethal intention, the calculation of the hunter intent on his kill.

"I had my own treasurer, a man trained by Victor-el-Tangier, but younger, a Moor, skilled in the ways of Frenchmen and others. He sucked the bones and brought them to me. Had it not been so serious, it would have been laughable. Victor-el-Tangier fell supinely into the trap."

Cruel! protested Diarmid. Uncle Victor had no guile. What he believed, he believed with the innocence of the child.

"When my father died, one evening, quite suddenly . . ."

Diarmid looked up but the impenetrable eyes were unblinking. He wondered: What — ? and was shocked by the blazing pride.

". . . all was in readiness. Majed-el-Tourin my brother summoned me from my apartments. I found my father breathing his last, clutching his bowels. He had been poisoned. By the English infidel."

"No!"

The Sheikh asked: "Do Englishmen never poison? It did not matter. My father was dead. I was the Sheikh."

"You did not— He was too innocent — "

"You knew this Englishman?"

Bleakly: "He was my uncle. He brought me up, together with my aunt. We guessed he had won a large fortune but where he had gone we never knew. We called it his 'final fling'."

"Ah!" Abou-el-Tourin eased himself more comfortably on his cushions. "He lives yet. A coincidence, Mr. Riall? I did not expect such a listener to my story. The good Allah works mysteriously when he sends me the nephew of the hated infidel to enthral with a tale of usury in our midst. You should be a novelist, to capture on the written page the frail nuances of this progression. It smacks of violence . . ."

"You harmed him?"

"A little. It was necessary to show the people how we were to continue. By rights, he should have had his head removed and displayed on the gate spikes."

Dear Mother of God! A bizarre fate, for the bookmaker's clerk . . .

"I spared him that. I took into account his expended service, his selfless devotion to my father. I knew he had not administered the poison. He was incarcerated, to repent of his wrongdoings, in a suite beneath the armoury, in every way a replica of his Treasurer's suite, with books and money. When he had found a way to triple the shekels, he would have his release. I would then believe his honesty, I told him. I could have decimated him and thrown him to the wolves. I could have removed his tongue, his hands and his eyes. I could have sliced off his ears or his toes. All good, clean Tourin methods for the braying of evil dogs. I did none of them. I respected my father's liking for the man. I gave him one slip of light and my father's spectacles to remind him he had little chance to outwit me. I fed him, sparingly, because the brain works better on an empty stomach, with nothing but his fingers to serve it and his teeth to dissect it. He took it," admiringly, "like a Moor. Indeed, he cringed less than a Moor. His head in a barboosh, he was conducted to his suite and allowed to ask for anything bar the things I had extenuated were not his. He asked for nothing.

"This year he proved to me that the shekels he had had could be tripled and I released him."

Deep, anguished pity was taking hold of him. "Can I be seeing him?" asked Diarmid.

"There is no penalty," said the Sheikh. "Victor-el-Tangier will juggle no more treasuries."

"You have not — ?"

"*Non*," lazily. "Neither I nor my retainers touched him bodily after he was conducted to his suite. He was alone, with his papers and his pencils. Sometimes I would stand in the doorway, to remind him I was waiting, that when he had accomplished his part of the bargain I would perform mine. He could go where he willed. He thanked me in his queer English intonation and said he was perfectly comfortable. He was spineless in captivity and I marvelled again that my father, a great sheikh, had seen a master in him."

"I find him — where?"

"In the bazaar, with the dogs, hanging

264

round the dig. I would not know. The episode of Victor-el Tangier served its purpose. My officials know what awaits them if they attempt similar feats of juggling. I have my fingers on my shekels. What matters it what has come to a single infidel with the heart gone from him?"

"I should try," began Diarmid. He eased his cramped limbs and endeavoured to ascertain the reason for the evening's "entertainment". Did Abou-el-Tourin usually enlighten his guests with stories of rapprochement and revenge? The features before him told him it was normal. This young man was a-thirst for power. In the struggle just commencing in his country it was he and his like who would mould its destiny with no assistance from the Victors or the French. "I feel ashamed that nobody ever attempted to find him."

"He was well hidden. One would not expect to find a bookmaker's clerk in the guise of a Palace Treasurer. Had you looked deep and well and used your excellent Scotland Yard, I hardly imagine you would have found him. My father, I might add, had his ways of protecting his protegées as well as warding off his sons."

"I can hardly believe it," said Diarmid. "Nothing I have ever imagined touches the actuality of the truth. Can you not set your men — ?"

"To catch the cur? Let the pack do that. I am occupied with more important matters. If you find him, I wish you joy of him. You may take him or leave him. The lesson has been learnt."

"You have no exception then," rising and standing before Abou-el-Tourin, "if he'd come, to his leaving Garraseesh?"

"For me he is nothing. I have amused myself with the tale of his pillory. It has passed an hour." He yawned. "Now, I have audiences." He lifted a bell by his side. "It has been a pleasure and I trust an enlightenment to relate to you certain events of my country. If you will take them with you when you leave and impart them in quarters where the stone gathers no moss I shall feel my efforts have been worthwhile. A great pity, dear sir, you did not go to Oxford. I always feel the university by the Isis has so much more to offer than the sluggish Cam-town. No offence," he said sweetly. "I am sure you view your own college in rosy light. It is just that my father's dark lenses await another owner and it interests me to guess at their wearer."

A servant had come in reply to the summons of the bell.

"Mohammed, convey Mr. Riall to the gates. We shall not have a similar pleasure, I am afraid. I leave tomorrow for Cairo on matters of state. You might intimate to that other infidel that my patience with his excavations is running low. If he cannot find any 'treasure', he too must be escorted, not to an underground suite, but to the first plane to leave for England. There is no time here to juggle with stones. The future is upon us; it demands that we act. Mosaics and pottery are not our need; weapons, friends, allies, men who have had awareness of the French and the English but not the Irish," smoothly. "You see, I differentiate."

On the high road outside the palace, Diarmid found no comfort in the heavy heat, nor in the glittering glare. Almost, he envisaged the impaled head of Victor Naismith grinning from a spike with wry shrewdness. Poor old chap! He had landed himself into a den of thieves.

The bundle of rags that hid the shape of a man shifted its position on the steps of the Great Mosque and stared myopically at the many feet passing to and fro. There was a great variety in the sandals. Priest and prime minister, sinner and sheikh, the sandals were as an open book to the bundle of rags that was the outward vestige of a man and when the spirit moved him he would compose a poem on their passage. In it no money ever stole; no breath of the coinage of privilege or pride was ever part of the odyssey that occupied the fertile brain of the bundle on the steps. It was a plaintive tune and after a time it palled, but the children sought in it couplets about Garraseesh which the poet knew as completely as they did. When they recognised it, they lingered, edging up the steps, hovering, to slide away with the rapidity of a cur if a priest or an official made his appearance. "Encore! Encore!" clapping their hands. Then the bundle would stir and hesitate and wrap the rags closer round and shrink into the stones.

The sandals of the grown-ups never ceased. They went up or down into the mosque and the bundle was nothing but a bundle that occasionally murmured strange notes that were neither Algerian nor Moorish.

One pair of sandals had stopped. That in itself was a contradiction. The eyes stared at the leather straps, the metal fasteners. There was something "other" about them. They weren't at all the normal sandals. He began to feel fear, a shivering in his spine that affected his hands and made them move supplicatingly over his knees. Then a thought came plaintively from a period in time, of sandals on a beach, spindly toes and a child laughing.

"Poor old chap," said a kind, gentle, murmuring voice with a hint of running water in it, as opposed to the rasping wails of his everyday existence. Long ago, he had heard a music like that, a young voice eager with joy shouting on the sands of Margate.

Margate! He began to extemporise, not quite sure of himself, bidden by the sandals stationary beside him.

"It was the fault of the office where you worked. Men won large fortunes and you did not see why you shouldn't, so you did some juggling and it was better than you thought, and that night Aunt Ma-Ma was harsh with you, reprimanding you for a dirty collar."

He whimpered like a dog. His body began to shiver and shake like a cur's.

"You thought you'd put your dreams into practice and have the devil of a lovely time. It was so easy. Aunt Ma-Ma was at her bridge drive and I was at the pictures and you just walked out. Walked out of St. John's Wood and reality and came to Garraseesh and was the Palace Treasurer."

"It was good while it lasted."

"What did you do in Tangier; and before that in Malta and Italy? Did you lay the foundations of your reputation? Did you do everything they said in *The Boys' Own Paper*?"

"It worked."

"Och, it worked," the crooning voice went on. "You became a great man. You went on juggling and then a clever young man came home from Paris and was a better juggler than you were and Victor-el-Tangier was hanging on by the skin of his teeth."

"Abdul-el-Tourin."

"Was good to you? God thank him for

it. I'll be remembering Abdul-el-Tourin but not Abou-el-Tourin. He's a cunning young man; he'll come to a sticky end. He won't sit on the steps of the mosque in Garraseesh, hugging his memories."

The toes with the sandals were wriggling in the heat. Once they had wriggled in the sea and Ma-Ma had stated . . .

"She never knew?"

"The depth of your fall? She would not be knowing about Victor-el-Tangier, high or low, Treasurer or prisoner. She is for lying in the cemetery with a white angel over her chest." There was a laughing tenderness in the voice which was on a level with his head. He saw that the sandals had almost disappeared beneath a pair of cotton khaki trousers. "She always liked white angels. Do you remember?"

"These chaps worship idols."

"Power and greed and war and ambition. We'll not be judging them too harshly. They're fighting for their existence, to make a country from a series of smaller territories. Somebody's got to go under. It's the way of the world. You knew that, in your heart. *The Boys Own Paper* only told of the glamour, Foreign Legion, sheikhs, palaces. You trod the marble floors. You were a Sheikh's trusted lieutenant. In the history of Algeria, you will be Victor-el-Tangier."

Loving, tender, amused and tolerant, surrounding him with its pity, coming to him through the uncomfortable heat, as a small boy had come once from Cloncobh in Ireland to wet the dryness of his days and fill the tall, narrow house with his gurgling laughter. "Would you like to be a sheikh, Uncle Victor?" He had been a Sheikh's Treasurer, in charge of the shekels. Treble them and you will be free. With Abdul-el-Tourin it would have been easy. A sheet of paper and a pencil. Rapid, magnificent sums and the elderly ruler would be radiant with joy. "Tell me again, Victor." His winning system. But with Abou-el-Tourin . . . there was nothing of his father in Abou-el-Tourin. He spotted the flaw, the only flaw. He had been to Oxford where a man learned to be wise and sagacious and oracular. It should have come out. In happiness it had come out. In captivity it refused to march to his will.

"Doesn't that always happen? Anything

is so much easier when one is content and in confidence. Take away the faith and everything is wrong. You tried, all those weary months; then you came here and the feet that had once stopped for you go by unheeding. It might have been worse."

But not much; he had been Victor-el-Tangier and he had ruled the palace with his infallible computations that he had learned in the bookmaker's office in Holborn. Easy computations, actually, a matter of repetition and slight adaptation.

"That arrogant young man should be a bookmaker. Maybe he will one day, when he comes a cropper, using the system of El-Tangier to recoup his losses. Then it won't have been in vain."

So it went on and he was lulled into a fitful doze and his head lolled forward until it was lost in the folds of the dirty rags and the sandals went up and down, the Algerian sandals, but the English pair did not go.

"Poor old chap. They punished you too harshly. They didn't know the beginning of it, when you sat in the sitting-room and filled a little boy with an eagerness to grasp the stars. That's what you were doing. You made him aware of the bright, big world. You told Aunt Ma-Ma not to chitter. That was your word — chitter. 'Don't chitter, Maisie. He's doing all right.' He is doing all right, Uncle Victor; he's going to see justice is done. He's going to Abou-el-Tourin to ask for a plane. You should have asked . . ." but one did not beg for mercy when one had been Victor-el-Tangier. First, though, he had to ensure . . . "Uncle Victor, will you be all right while I go and make the arrangements? I couldn't be making them until I had found you but now that I have . . ."

The bundle had slipped sideways. It was not aware when the sandals went away quickly . . . and it wasn't there when they returned, with a taxi.

"Where is he? Victor-el-Tangier? The man who sat here. Has he gone home? Would you be telling me where he lives?"

A swarthy-faced Moor condescended to reply.

"He was dead. He has been taken for burial. One has to hurry the burial here in this heat. You may find him . . ."

The sandals that were different went back down the steps and along the crowd-

274

ed, dusty street. Perhaps it was as well. Victor-el-Tangier could not have gone back to Victoria Road or anywhere else in the London that had taught him his craft. He was part of this foreign, exotic, Algerian scene where he had spent the most glorious and the most pathetic days of his life.

What a final fling!

THEY went back to London and Diarmid refused to do Effie Clanrobin's Moorish palace. It was the first commission he had turned down but he was adamant; the evening he had spent with Abou-el-Tourin forbade any question of creating such a setting while the tragedy of Victor Naismith was fresh in their minds. When, two months later, a news report from Algeria said there had been fighting in Garraseesh and Abou-el-Tourin had been superseded in his sheikhdom by his brother Majed it made no material difference. He had been too clever and too confident and he was paying, as Victor-el Tangier had paid; the counters had not run straight when he tried to juggle with them. He was now wearing his father's dark spectacles and another ruler sat on the silken cushions.

"I wish you had never gone," Marcia said. She had invited him to Winter's Grace, thinking the quiet country scene would lull the pain. Anne-Louise and Sean were there but they had no eyes for another's ache; they were concerned solely with themselves.

"Father likes him," she said.

They were seated in the hall, before a roaring fire. The young people had gone out in Sean's new green racing car which he had bought with his gratuity, exploring the byways and lanes.

"He is the type to succeed in the City — and has the charm to wheedle a financier. I'm growing a little fonder of my nephew now that Anne-Louise is rubbing the sharp edges off him."

"I wish I knew whether it was good for her."

Diarmid stroked the idle hand. "Darling, he said, "you can't be arranging others' lives for them. It's just what Anne-Louise wants, after the upset of her transition here. They've both seen the world."

"From the safe lea of her father's mission."

"Admittedly," he pulled her on to his knee, "his experience is greater than hers. He's much less touchy, don't you think?

Hector says he sat two hours with him last week and criticised *The Sycamore Square* with the grasp of an expert. He'll be challenging men like Rossington and Cassell before he's even grown a beard."

"Diarmid, he isn't — ?"

"I heard Anne-Louise saying she liked men with beards. Is that them now? You'd better send for tea. They'll be ravenous. Hallo, Anne-Louise," as the girl came in through the front door. "'Tis blooming you look, all the frost and glitter on your nose. Sean, my lad, close the door. Brr!" He shook himself.

"We've been to Honeymede Hill," said Anne-Louise.

"Was it the most marvellous view in the world?" lightly.

"I saw you there," said Sean. He was standing beside Anne-Louise, quick to scent criticism, with a look of Padraig in his bog-dark eyes, "when I came back from Chatterley."

"Diarmid's always going there," said Marcia. "He looks for ideas."

"Do you?" asked Anne-Louise. She was like a spring flower, dispensing her fragrance. "What is it next time?"

"Nothing," laughed Diarmid. "I've no commission pending."

"Only *The Sycamore Square*," put in Sean.

"Was your mother well?" Diarmid asked him. He must get to know this boy, if Anne-Louise were serious, and every part of her proclaimed her to be. Could he, in a year or two, reconcile him to Padraig, take him to Marchmont? "Tell Anne-Louise about the dig," to Marcia. "She said she wanted to come."

"Please." Anne-Louise dropped on her haunches before the fire. "Will the Professor have me, Marcia? Sean, don't growl! Because your father won't speak to you doesn't mean I can't go. I'll soften his heart so he'll send for you, darling. Anyway," with supreme logic, "I can't say whether I shall like it until I've seen it. Diarmid tells me it's wild."

"Too wild for a flower like you."

"I'm tough."

"To live at Marchmont you have to be tougher than that." His gaze slid round to the erect young man. The impossible twist to the position! The son of Padraig in love with Anne-Louise. Of all young men with whom she might have fallen in love, it had to be Sean ... and he, Diarmid, had caused it to happen. "It's time to be telling you a history of Marchmont, Anne-Louise, so you don't fall into the bog and get yourself drowned."

"I can swim," twinkled Anne-Louise.

Not like the Waldsteins, he thought.

"If there's any telling to be done," said Sean quickly, "it's myself will be doing it."

"You don't know it all," said Diarmid. His tone had a kill in it, a note Marcia had never heard before, which caused her to lift her head swiftly. I will be doing it, he stated, across the uplifted head of Anne-Louise; I will be calling on the little people and make their presence known; I will be going again to Cuimin's island and taking Sean with me who is a Riall and the son of Padraig Riall, whether he wishes it or no; I will be telling him of his father and Kirsty and the Book of Cuimin and the whole wild series of events because some poor soul has to do it before we are caught again in the tentacles of Marchmont.

"Come for a walk, Sean," he said when tea was over. "The dogs need exercise."

He pulled on his thick winter coat and took a stick from the stand.

Sean followed. "Why — ?" he began.

"There's plenty of time to spend with Anne-Louise."

"I promised — " the boy said.

"Listen, Sean. I'll be telling you about Padraig." He ignored the straining away, the sullen expression that came into the obstinate features, the lifting, protesting anger. "You have heard your mother's side. I'm saying your mother's an isolated woman. I'm not agreeing with what she's done; that doesn't enter into it. What she is and what has come out of her actions is what concerns us now."

"She's been ill-treated," roughly.

"So has Padraig. She it was who ran away to London. From the best of motives, I assure you. She didn't want to be a drag on him; she was frightened; she saw in Alice Shane an escape from a situation into which she had been pulled. Your father made her go to the city, implored her with the tears in his eyes. He was unhappy, unsure; his father had stabbed him. For sure, two hurts don't make a peace. If you go on nursing a grudge you'll be damaging the lovely relationship with Anne-Louise. Love cannot live with hatred. That is where your father's been making his mistake." There was the example of Victor-el-Tangier to hold before the gaze. "Listen, my dear," as they trudged along the narrow woodland path, "to a cautionary tale," and he recounted it, without ornament, so that the futility and the truth hovered in the winter air. Sean stared deliberately ahead. Every now and then his throat worked but otherwise he was quiet until Diarmid finished. "He was dead when I got back. I'm not wanting to go to Marchmont and finding your father dead also."

"There's no connection— That other man, Uncle Victor," with something of surprise as the kinship of the abandoned bundle of rags became clear to him, "had his fling."

"That's what I'm afraid of, Sean. When a man's driven too far, he grasps for the impossibility, the fame and the grandeur he has missed, only then it is warped and off-balance. Can't you see — ?"

"I cannot see," declared Sean. "I am going to work for Sir Bruno. I am going to marry Anne-Louise. You cannot stop me."

"I am not wanting to stop you. I am very happy that Anne-Louise loves you. I want you to realise the good fortune you have gained."

"You needn't croak . . ."

How the young spat! Seeing danger in every approach. Determined to guard their privileges with sword-drawn stance. As it should be, Diarmid insisted. He wished Hector had been here, to explain the analogy, put into clear straight-forward English the problems to be faced.

He returned to Padraig. "In the summer he wrote me a letter, an appeal. I went and found him distressed. Professor Codrill and Marcia were there with the team, and he was obsessed with the idea that he should forbid Clunare. Your mother has told you about the saints, about her going to St. Cuimin and regaining her strength. That should have been the occasion of their reunion. Instead," he felt the boy tense and harden his heart against the recounting, "he shut his eyes. Don't be blaming your father out of hand, Sean. Don't be forgetting he had long years of ache and frustration, of exaggerating the schism. He was overawed by the miracle, seeing in it a condemnation of his behaviour."

"He was cruel," shrilly.

"I agree. A man is cruel when he is hurt. He lashes at all innocent things, and your mother was not innocent. You are a man, Sean. You can appreciate these facts. Put yourself in his place, imagine for a moment that Anne-Louise . . ."

He thought the boy would strike him; but he had got through, beneath the outer skin, pricked the heart that beat furiously within. Desperately, he drove home his advantage.

"The dig will be resumed when the weather improves. Anne-Louise wants to go, and Marcia has half-promised her."

"I shall be working," starkly.

"By then, you could have a few days off. There's a very soft spot in Sir Bruno's heart for Anne-Louise."

"I'll not ask — " firmly.

"I was hoping you would, but if you won't — " He let it be, slashing with his stick at an overhanging twig. "There's so much there one hasn't unravelled, one feels one ought not to give up."

"Why not ask Father O'Rourke?"

"Is it a matter for Father O'Rourke? Or for Sir Eric Frost? It's in the relationship of men and women, in the feelings in their hearts, in the acts they perform when they're full of anger and heat. Then is the time to take a knife and cut into the centre, as Hector did in *The Irish Room*, but . . ." He trailed off. This talk was leading him into a morass as wet and sticky as the bogs beyond Kilmeenan. Not even Father O'-Rourke's implicit faith could extradite them from the welter of sludge . . . "We'd best be leaving it, Sean, and go back to the fire. I felt a need to explain . . ." He shrugged his shoulders. Too many years with Kirsty had set this boy against a solution.

"It's not that I don't want — "

"You don't want — ?" he encouraged.

"In faith, Uncle Diarmid," the choking voice broke out, "it's hard to be the core of a dispute like that. When I wasn't for knowing about him, it was nothing, but Mother said, after Cuimin and Clunare, and I've hated him since — "

"She should have told you that it was not his fault entirely."

"She did," he admitted with reluctance.

285

"Och, then — "

"It was his fault."

"He pleaded for her love and being the woman she was she gave it to him."

"You're on her side now."

"I'm on the side that is going to bring this cleft to an ending. I can't stand by and see Padraig pushed out of life; I can't condemn as unworthy what your mother has done. I sent for her for Hector . . ." He sighed. "You'll be saying to remove her from Dunphilly. Actually, I could think of no one else. She's pleased Hector. You wouldn't be blaming me, Sean, for asking her to come? You met Anne-Louise in Waddesdon Square," placing his hand on the young, sharp shoulder. "We're all in this. We cannot help it. Circumstances have been too great for us. You know the story from both sides, though as yet you haven't seen Padraig."

"I have seen him."

"But not met him, spoken to him, touched him? I'm not asking you to judge," softly. "In faith, who could judge, unless it be St. Cuimin himself? What I am asking you is whether, if the need arose, you'd help me."

The other was silent, staring mutely at the line of hills which divided the sky-line at the end of the padded path. All his nature shied from that which he was being asked, all his emotions centred fully and conclusively on Anne-Louise and his employment with Waldstein's. He had cut adrift; he was facing the future; it was clear . . .

"Don't say now," went on Diarmid. "It's a big thing I'm asking. Sleep on it; think about it; don't do anything that you'll regret. It's just that, the Rialls being affected — "

"I'll not promise," he said. The warring showed on his tested face.

"That's the man! Promises have to be kept. Good heavens! It's five o'clock! Marcia and Anne-Louise will be wondering where we are. It's a fine view, Sean, but so it is towards Clunare."

"Diarmid!"

Marcia came running as they entered the hall. "There was a personal call from London just after you left. I did not know which way you'd gone. They're ringing again at half-past five."

It was then a quarter past.

"Some countess in a tizzy." He closed the door. "Chester can usually deal with them but occasionally he finds it beyond him."

"It it's urgent, you'll have to go."

He caught her hand. "Bless you."

When the phone rang, it was Hector. "Diarmid? There's trouble at Marchmont. Kirsty's had a wire from Seamus Macroom. The Book's missing."

"In faith! I thought it was kept under lock and key."

"So it was. Seamus had the key; but it's gone from his ring. Whoever rifled the Old Library knew their way about, but Kirsty says that's practically everybody. The Library's open to all, whether they study or not, and the Book's been creating a pretty storm, with articles in the paper by your brother."

"Well," reasonably, "it's the obvious, isn't it? He's the owner of Marchmont."

"Don't haver, Diarmid," Hector retorted. "Kirsty thinks it's suspicious."

"Anything Padraig did would be suspicious to her. I've just been talking to Sean. He's awkward. He won't see eye for an eye or tooth for a tooth. I'm washing my hands of them and concentrating on my career."

Hector's small chuckle was brief. "You won't be saying that very long. Kirsty wants you to go. She's going too. She regards the loss of the Book of Cuimin as a serious affair."

" 'Tis that, indeed. Who does she think has it? Himself? In the fastness of Marchmont or on Clunare? I'm happy here, Hector. I'm warm and cosy and the air's frosty and inspiring. In Ireland it'll be raining and the mist will be raw. We're going with Codrill in March. Padraig will look after the Book," but a queer, sickly, unhappy emotion was beginning to clutch at his vitals. Padraig had a "fix" on Clunare; he was not himself when he thought about it; it had to do with their mother and Kirsty and a host of other things. "It's his, after all; it was only on loan; he let the college have it for the summer; he may want to study it at leisure, seek a formula from it for a history . . . What's Kirsty about? She can't throw herself at him and have the knife attack her again. She can't want to go to Marchmont. It's not reasonable. It's a woman all over," he complained.

"She thinks Padraig may be in danger."

"From what? Sir Eric didn't think so."

"She says the Book's a holy book and if you're living in his country . . ."

"You look at it with his eyes? All right. I'll ring Sir Eric. Then I'll get back to you. Will you be telling her . . ."

He dialled the number of the specialist and found him at home.

"This is Diarmid Riall speaking. You visited my brother in December. We're afraid he's in some trouble. The Book of Cuimin — you know, it was found on Clunare and he gave it to the Library for safe keeping — it's missing and Kirsty O'Halloran — you recollect, she and Padraig . . . she thinks he may have taken it and be hoarding it. He has queer notions about Clunare because of a series of events. I discussed them with you. Would you be thinking there's any danger?"

"I would advise you to go to see," promptly.

"Och!" Then: "I was thinking so too." He turned over in his mind the contracts he had on hand. Chester could cope. "I'll be making the arrangements then."

"You'll keep in touch? If it's necessary I'll come over."

"Thank you, Sir Eric." He put down the receiver. "Sean, ring up your mother and tell her I'm off to the Royal. She'll know why." Then he hurried in search of Marcia. "Darling, Padraig's in distress. He's taken the Book of Cuimin."

"Not destroyed it?"

"I'm not for knowing. I'm going to see."

"I'll come with you," at once.

"Bless you." He kissed her. "It may be a wild goose chase. Kirsty's anxious. She had a telegram from Seamus Macroom."

"She's not going — ?"

"She is. I can't fathom the logic of a woman's mind. She leaves him when he has nobody else to look after him; now when he's lived half his life she's going back. She must go, she says. Oh, Pratt's well enough to leave. Hector tossed that in. She'd have gone, without that. There's something in the wind, more than the Book . . ."

"I'll be ready in half an hour."

"We'll meet Kirsty at Paddington. She's

booking our seats on the train and getting us passages."

"What about Sean? Did you achieve anything on your walk?"

"Nothing much. He's on to Kirsty now. If she says come, he'll learn more in a few hours. If he doesn't— Marcia, he must work out his own equation."

"He mustn't hurt Anne-Louise," quickly.

"I have a feeling Anne-Louise can look after herself in a matter of saints and such like. She had a missionary for a father."

6

THEY sat in the train, the five of them, he and Marcia, Sean, Anne-Louise, and Kirsty, and the strain of their journey was on their faces and in the way they held themselves.

"What do you think?" Marcia asked. As she had feared, Anne-Louise had insisted on coming once Sean had said: "I'm with you, Uncle Diarmid." This affected her as much as it affected them, more because she loved Sean and she was not sure that the others did; apart from Kirsty, that was. She was watching Kirsty now, as Marcia asked: "What do you think?"

"I think he's for hurting himself," said Kirsty stonily.

Diarmid agreed. "He's been hurting himself ever since he went with you."

"This is a punishment," said Kirsty, "for what I have done."

Nonsense, Marcia's modern mind reacted. Actually, she replied: "He cut you out. Until then, maybe; after that, no. If he's come to harm, it's because he's no longer responsible for his acts." She defied them to deny her. "Why won't you acknowledge it? Never mind what Sir Eric said. He was thinking of the guineas. He can quite easily say the situation has deteriorated. We shouldn't have let him remain there. We're all to blame. Except Anne-Louise," squeezing the small, pale hand with passion. "We've all been so busy chasing our own fancies that we've forgotten his are veiled. The dig set in motion a series of matters in his mind that must have been smouldering for years. We should have seen it. We should have done so if we had not been so excited with the scrolls and the Book. St. Cuimin could see it," astonishingly.

"Marcia — "

She turned to him defiantly. "Well, don't you attribute your saint with exceptional foresight? Didn't you believe he had cured you, Kirsty? It's this credulousness of the Irish that's to blame. Darling, I love you for it, but somebody has to be rational. Your clever Hector can't come; he's an invalid; but at least some of us have imbibed his common sense. He says an ulcer is in the relationships of man. Wasn't that his theme in *The Irish Room*? But those relationships were as nothing to this one we have now on our hands. It is serious, Diarmid, so serious we may not get there in time." She was looking at Kirsty and saw the blood drain out of her cheeks. "Kirsty knows. She hasn't said so, because of Sean and Anne-Louise, but now they're with us they'll have to know. Sean must face the fact that his father has done this thing because his mother deserted him. I'm not talking nonsense, Diarmid, nor have I been listening to Sir Eric; I've been taking every small fact as I would a piece of ceramic and examining it. It's all there, clearer than the names of the abbots on the scrolls, far clearer than any words St. Cuimin wrote in his book. We've been looking at the wrong pieces. If we had not been so blinded by the Latin and the antiquity, we'd have seen this thing coming and attempted to avoid it." She threw her words, definite, intent, into the railway carriage and they reacted in their several ways.

" 'Tis the truth," said Kirsty; her figure

had lost some of its buoyancy. "He was jealous of my studying with Seamus. He saw in it an attempt to claim Cuimin — "

"Kirsty, you came away!"

"Leaving the path clear."

"You should have told me — " Diarmid was concerned with the struggle in Sean's eyes, the tightly clenched hands, the tense, gripped lips. What a homecoming for the boy!

"And you off to Algeria, begorra, to find that poor thing."

"I didn't expect to find him," but in Uncle Victor's case was a clue to this other, if it could be grasped. What had he said to Sean? "When a man is repressed, he seeks other ways to assert himself." Victor-el-Tangier? The taking of Cuimin's Book? In Padraig's eyes there was no greater treasure, unearthed on Clunare and deposited in an alien library. Never mind that he had placed it there himself. When it was threatened by Kirsty O'Halloran . . . He glimpsed vaguely the workings of the oppressed mind, the need for revenge, the gloating, cunning, importunate decision. There was no Professor to advise him, to protest: "It should be protected," no denim-trousered diggers to complicate the issue. He was alone. At the altar of a man who had chosen the solitary life, he could lay his throbbing head. "I am glad I found him," he said, shaken. "I have learned from Uncle Victor, but it was Padraig I should have written instead of telling Sean." Apologising, he requested pardon of the woman who had shared an uneasy union. "I should have seen, when I came to visit you . . . but I was intent on *The Irish Room*, beguiled away from the task he had given me. He was wanting me near. In faith," he jumped up, unable to bear the conclusion, and paced the carriage jerkily, "I had the example; I could have eased it, had I paused."

"Diarmid, you tried. You gave nearly every minute — " said Kirsty. She was seeing his distress and would have comforted him, save there was no comfort until they arrived at Marchmont, and possibly not then . . .

"I did not give every minute. I should have known, on Clunare, when he nearly drowned himself, when he found the list. The Book should have stayed. It was sacred. It's my responsibility. I lifted it out and gave it to him. I gave him the agony."

"Diarmid, my dear — " said Kirsty.

"You told me about the Book." He turned on her. "You said Cuimin had it."

"So he had."

"If you hadn't told me, I wouldn't have expected to find it. I wouldn't have credited to Cuimin the power that I did. I had escaped. Now . . ."

"You are going to help Padraig," said Anne-Louise, her young face soft and serious. "If I was in trouble" — she stared hard at Sean who would not meet her appeal— "I'd rather have you than anybody else."

His lips trembled. "Alanna, you don't know." He shouted roughly: "I've made it worse, delving into the history, reminding him when he wanted to forget, going to see Kirsty."

"I told you my heart."

"It's Padraig's heart we now have to find."

"Aren't we losing our sense of proportion?" That was Marcia. "Padraig may be all right, sitting in his library, examining the pages."

His lips quivered. " 'Tis a wonderful

book but you have to know the Latin to read it."

"We can all read Latin," said Sean.

Diarmid sat down. He brushed his hand across his brow. "We shall have need of it before we're through, I am thinking."

The stationmaster was on the platform when they got out of the train at Dunphilly. He raised his hat to Diarmid and Marcia and Kirsty.

"You're welcome," he said.

"Have they found the Book?"

He smiled at Sean — often in his youth Sean had spent excited hours in the signalman's box and in the stationmaster's office — and noted the fair English girl who stood at his side.

"This is Anne-Louise, Mr. McEwan," introduced Sean, recovering his manners. He was pinched and strained but the friendliness of his old mentor thawed a little of the chill.

"How do you do," said Anne-Louise.

"A very good day to you," said Mr. McEwan. It was obvious he approved of her. In the midst of their stress, Kirsty noted the twinkle beginning to gleam beneath the grey brows. "The Book's not found yet, Mr. Riall, but Superintendent Mulligan's of the opinion it's at Marchmont. I see you're in favour of that too."

"We've come to find it," said Diarmid. "You haven't seen my brother lately? I'd have been here before . . ."

"Och, we saw the notices of *The Irish Room*. We knew Mrs. O'Halloran was off to be housekeeper to the author. She told us that, Mr. Riall. 'Tisn't often the news of society reaches Dunphilly."

"Is there a car available? We're going to Marchmont."

Mr. McEwan shook his head sadly. "A sick man, Mr. Padraig, I'll be fearing, with a burden on his mind. There was a time when we thought he'd do well, go for a professor or a tutor at Trinity, with his Latin and his languages and his fine, high brow, and make the name of Riall admired in these parts. I know his mother wanted it. 'Mr. McEwan', she said to me more than the once, 'he's going to be my star. He's got the mind to lift Marchmont from these mists and give it a shine'. A dear, good lady, your mother, Mr. Diarmid, begging your pardon for not referring to your own good name."

"Whereas I am the one who's made the name of Riall known and he's sunk in the slough."

"Aye, the promise went dull somewhere." He did not look at Kirsty. Behind him Anne-Louise held Sean's hand and pressed it tightly.

"There's Pat Keogh can run you to Marchmont, if you'll not be having fears of the cab."

"Anything will do so long as we get there. Should we see Seamus or Superintendent Mulligan?"

"The Superintendent's over at the Royal, Pat was for telling me not half an hour ago."

"Then, for heavens' sake . . ." cried Diarmid.

They piled into Pat Keogh's cab. It was old and the seats were losing their stuffing but they gave little notice to that. They rattled through the town and passed the house in Christy Street where Kirsty lived. She gave Diarmid a half-lidded glance which said: If I had chosen Padraig and not Amos Brierley . . . but it was too late. Filled with anxiety, they urged Pat Keogh to hurry faster; never mind the springs, begod; never mind the tyres; a man's existence was in forfeit.

Last time he had come this way with Padraig, hoping to know the man whom he had last seen when a boy in the war . . . and knew he had gained no knowledge during the time he had been at the Royal. As he had never known Uncle Victor until he saw him a huddled bundle of rags on the steps of the mosque. "Poor old chap." His gentleness and acceptance had given peace to the final blurred moments.

He sat forward on the seat as they careered towards Marchmont. The last corkscrew bend into the village, skimming the high hedged banks, the skid of the wheels as a hen flew squawking from Kirsty's native cottage, the glimpse of her white face, her blind courage, her moral atonement, the glimpse of the Royal through the bare trees, Anne-Louise (she was going to help the boy, assist him to overcome the barriers he had erected between himself and this place) saying: "It's lovely," and thanking her wordlessly for being young enough and brave enough to come to the tragedy they might find with that high trust, Marcia upright and frank, having put them on the right road, coming to him that first evening across the hall, Sean . . . This was nasty for Sean; but there was nothing they could do; he was face to face with his beginning; in the way he approached it was the hope or the failure of his love for Anne-Louise.

"Mother — "

"You should be here, Sean."

"I shall hate him," flatly.

"My darlint," she answered. Without evasion or fabrication, Kirsty's southern voice fell into the well of the cab. "Nobody hates him, the poor lost soul. 'Tis where he made his mistake. We loved him, alanna, his brightness, his waywardness, his promise and his weakness; we loved him too much and thought to do him least harm by running away. God forgive us, my son. We should have stayed; we should not have ruined his hopes; we should have made his rooms cosy and warm. Even the second time we should have taken him, cruel spite and all, shown him what St. Cuimin showed. I am a wicked woman, methinks — "

"You are not," hoarsely, but he could not urge his throat to produce the denial. The muscles pressed achingly and the hard youthful face fought with the stern necessity for statement, but his mouth was useless, dry and dumb. Mistily, he blinked his eyelids, forcing them to look at the home of his father, and could not see it for the emotions and wild passions threshing inside him.

"A woman should not leave her man defenceless," in a low, parched whisper. "You hear that, Anne-Louise? If you want to go, once having taken him, you should not. You should endure hell and beyond and be humble to the end. St. Cuimin had the words. *'Be faithful to your God and He is merciful'*. Begod," she moaned, holding herself in the clasp of her distress, "I turned away and was thinking to wait. God has been merciful in that I am here, with my heart in the ground, bowing my head . . ." They hearkened, wonderingly, each feeling the abasement and the sorrow and the hard bitter knowledge. "He will be another Padraig," with a painful, twisting smile. "The marks will be on him. Pride will harden the smoothness, position garner the kicks. It is my doing, I say; I am sorry, my dear. I should have had more faith, more stout-heartedness . . ."

"I love him," said Anne-Louise. She had no fear. She would take Sean and hold him to her heart and know the future was hers.

"They will learn," murmured Kirsty. Then she looked at Diarmid. He was blood of Sean's blood, kin of her kin. "It was the same, listening to Padraig. The smooth, persisting tongue! The wholeness of his dependency! I could not refuse him. If he had called once, in all these years, I would have come. I came to Dunphilly; I met him in the street; I was always hoping . . ."

"Kirsty, he must have known — "

"He is learning, the wild boy, on the stones of Clunare; he is bending his ear to the ghostly voice that is carried on the high wind and in the grasses and comes back from the quick, scudding clouds . . ."

A gust of wind caught the cab and caused it to lurch. Diarmid was aware that the hedges were shaking, the trees in the approach to the Royal were bent with a fierce fury. They had turned in by the gate posts and Pat Keogh was wrenching at the wheel, all the time hearing Kirsty half-talking to herself, half-saying . . .

"Kirsty, you're not thinking — ?"

"Aren't you, Diarmid?" she rejoined.

Och, that he was; and Marcia too. Her strained features were on his other side; she was listening to Kirsty's low, penetrating voice with a side-by-side knowledge in her eyes, though hers were English and brown, and Kirsty's were Irish and grey.

"We'll be after him," he said and felt the wind dragging at his coat as he stepped down from the cab. With a resounding crash that shuddered their ears, an oak came splintering down on the edge of the lawn, sending its fractured branches across the grass.

"Holy Mother of God!" said Pat Keogh.

Kirsty took his arm. "It is the way, Diarmid. Don't thresh so. If he is there, the saint will be with him. I know that St. Cuimin is there. No dig can bring him out of Clunare. That is Cuimin's isle and there you put yourself in Cuimin's care."

"Mother, you said — " Sean pushed his way forward. "On a day like this nobody would venture to Clunare. Even my father," he gulped, "has enough sense to see — "

"At last the sense to see— There is the

Superintendent, Diarmid," as the front door opened and the figure of the policeman was framed in the doorway.

"I thought I heard a car." Superintendent Mulligan came down the steps. "Though with that crash I couldn't be sure."

"It's an oak," said Diarmid, "on the edge of the lawn." He went forward. "Seamus Macroom wired to Mrs. O'Halloran."

"Come in," said the Superintendent. "I'm remaining till the wind has died down. Then we can get across. You'll be knowing Mr. Riall's there, with the Book ?"

"We'll be knowing," replied Diarmid.

They went into the study. Books lay about in a tumultuous disarray. Papers were strewn on the desk and on chairs. The bureau stood open.

"I found it like this," said Superintendent Mulligan.

"The poor dear darlint," breathed Kirsty.

Marcia began to collect the jumbled papers and put them into tidy piles. It gave her something to do and occupied her hands while the policeman told Diarmid and Kirsty what he knew. Another pair of hands began to help her, Anne-Louise's, shaking a little, unsure, every now and then pausing as Sean's angry, hesitant steps approached and moved away as he trod the worn carpet.

" 'Faith," cried Diarmid once, "will you be stopping that?"

Sean halted abruptly. He mumbled an apology; then started again, unable to hold his limbs in abeyance with his mind. "I've never seen it — " he began.

"Come and help," called Anne-Louise but he shied away, guarded, distraught.

"I wouldn't touch them!"

"If anything's happened to him," Marcia said, "they'll be yours."

He hadn't got that far. His horror, his dismay and his sonship were mixed up in his chaotic heart. His love for Anne-Louise, miraculous and magical, like a stream in the countryside, warred with his tensile memory of his mother after Amos. He had held it, naked, sharp as a knife, never losing the edge of it; and now his mother had turned full circle. She said she was loving the hated man, the cause of her grief. No wonder he paced, back and forth, blind to Anne-Louise's beseechings, Marcia's steady reasonableness.

"Sean — " said Kirsty.

He flung up his head. He was like an animal at bay, baring its teeth, fearing death. Never had they, in that room, seen such a griped pain as came out of Sean's hard-pressed inner torment.

"Mrs. Sullivan can tell you how he sat in here, with the Book, for five whole days, until the wind began to blow and the sea lashed the rocks below the Reek and a fury got into him," said the Superintendent.

"The wish of St. Cuimin. I know it myself," Kirsty said. "It calls and there's no refusing it. He'd go, in his suit and all, with no overcoat, and take Donal Murphy's boat and pull across the bay."

"He'd be drowned," put in Diarmid. He was grey and gaunt, limp with the weariness of the journey, the absence instead of the presence at the Royal. "There's no chance with the bay in that turmoil. Donal told me; he knows. Have you seen Donal?"

"He did his best, Mr. Diarmid. He took hold of the stern and tried to hold it but Mr. Padraig was determined; he pushed him away with the strength of your father,

Donal said, and shipped the oars and pulled away, laughing and shouting: 'I'm away to Clunare, Donal, and there's no one to stop me. Cuimin's calling. He wants his book back.' "

"Ah!" That was Kirsty. "He'd learned the lesson! To rob is to be damned."

"I took the Book," said Diarmid bleakly.

"A great treasure, the Book," said Superintendent Mulligan, "wasted in that broken altar. You did the right thing, Mr. Diarmid, and there's nothing to judge you in your doing. There's a festering in Mr. Padraig's mind and he has to eject it, like Mrs. O'Halloran says. Had the de'il not taken it into his head to blow and uproot that tree and send his breakers crashing on the beach at Cloncobh, we'd have been over there and found him and put him to bed. There's a poison in this de'il, Mr. Diarmid, halting strong men from pursuing their duty. Donal, he tried, but he was sent flying to the ground, with two ribs stove in. Away to Dunphilly they took him. Nobody else would try, though the crone from the churchyard said he was in his grave alongside his mother. I'll not be thinking that, Mr. Diarmid. He's a tough nut, Mr.

Padraig, for all his gulled fancies, and he knows Clunare and he knows the bay; there'll be no more harm than a choked lung; but I'd be wishing I could reach him, the same. The rapscallion, he is, calling me like this and making me helpless. For sure, if I thought there was any danger I'd have notified you, Mr. Diarmid, but it didn't occur to me until they took Donal to Dunphilly that we were in for a long stretch, and when I saw this I was for saying to myself: 'The man's a fool, to go out on a day with the wind. Riall or no Riall, it's putting too great a strain on the Almighty to allow a frail craft like Murphy's boat to float in this hurricane; but I'm thinking now, when you said he was near to drowning in the summer on a tide nothing as wild as this, that he's not so strong as he was, that the things he has on his mind have weakened him . . ."

"For God's sake," protested Sean, "can't we do something? I'll go mad if I stay here any longer. Can't I try — ?" His mother's face was a torture to him. His whipcord body, made in the mould of previous Rialls, edged for release from his caging. "I'm a good swimmer. I can row."

"You'd go to your death," Diarmid said sharply.

"Have patience," advised Marcia. "As soon as the wind drops, the Superintendent will try. Diarmid, shall I find Mrs. Sullivan? We've had no refreshment."

He shot her a thankful, admiring glance. "Hot coffee and rum. It'll do us all good. Marcia's right, Sean. No one could live in this turmoil."

"I'm going to try!"

"Sean," said Kirsty.

"It's not human to stand here, if he's out there." Now it was said; the struggle in his heart had resolved itself into a necessity to save the man whose absence was draining his mother of vitality. "You can't think so," angrily to Anne-Louise. "You didn't run away when your father died. I'm not running away now." His breath caught in his throat. "I'm not running from my responsibilities. He's my father, whatever he's done, and he's not going to die without I try . . . Mother, you must listen! You must hear me out! You've brought me to Marchmont. You've shown me where he lives, what he is. You can't say 'Wait' now I've made up my mind to find him. You can't say anything," shrilly, the sentences torn from him in a cavalcade of misery. "I don't want to see him; I don't want to speak to him; but he's my father. God in heaven, why you ever made him my father I don't know but it's too late to alter it, when he's in danger. I won't have it said I ran out on him too. I've heard enough said today to make me want to choke him but I've also heard enough said to want to tell him I'm here. I want one day to have a son and what am I going to say to *him*? That I didn't go to my father when he was in trouble? That I was too heartless to do anything more than trample a piece of carpet?"

"You'll break your mother's heart," said Diarmid.

"She hasn't cared much about mine. She hasn't thought that a son wants his father, that whatever he is and whatever he's done — "

"I cannot tell him not to go," whispered Kirsty. She was swiftly aged and grey. Impulsively, Anne-Louise went towards her. She took the limp, lined hand and held it. In her light, caressing voice, she said: "I want him to go, Mrs. O'Halloran."

The swaying figure shivered. "You do not — " Then a fraction of the stout courage came back to Kirsty's bearing. She took the girl in her arms and hugged her tightly.

"Perhaps St. Cuimin will give a thought to him, Anne-Louise. There was a prayer in the Book. '*Look kindly on the young, O Lord, and save them from their headstrongness*'. I found the Latin very difficult. All the worthwhile things are difficult. When you find him, Sean, tell him — "

"I'll tell him — what I want to tell him," shakily.

WITH the dawn came a lessening of the gale. The sky was clear and a weak sun shone down on the ancient stone house and the wreckage about its walls. Through the gap between the Pins and the Reek, the island of Clunare showed clear and blue, a hallowed place wherein was sanctity and solitude and a solving of one's problems. On the beach below the white-washed stone cottage of Donal Murphy a knot of people was standing as a boat came slowly across the bay.

Kirsty O'Halloran stood apart and in this moment of reckoning there was no one to deny her her solitariness. Once it had been she who had come from the sea, cured and iridescent, and the watching one had cursed her and caused the years of apartness. Now it was she who was watching, wrapped in her long tweed coat, her gaze on the heaving waters, in her mind what thoughts and concessions and on her features the strain of her long night's suffering. Two people the boat was bringing her, but there was nothing in her to know what the outcome might be, save that she was praying with the whole of her soul for help in this meeting.

Not far away but beyond speaking distance stood Marcia and Anne-Louise, every now and then sending their anxious, wordless glances in her direction, holding each other's courage in the palms of their hands, clinging to each other for comfort in this morning hour when every part of their known world was affected.

"Marcia, I'm afraid," whispered Anne-Louise.

"So am I, Anne-Louise." For Diarmid and for Sean and for Padraig. For the Rialls who were coming to their muster in the bleakness of this western cove. As Rialls before them had come.

Would it not be better to abandon the dig, forsake these Irish saints and their faded parchments, go in search of the sun in Greece or Turkey? Diarmid would need sunshine after this.

She saw him in the boat, with the Superintendent, bending his heaving shoulders to the oars, acting as attendant or as pall-bearer to his brother and his nephew.

"It'll be all right," she said, but where was the guarantee? The bay on a night like last night was no normal challenge to a boy in distress.

"If anything's happened to Sean — " muttered Anne-Louise, staring miserably at the boat and moving like one in a dream to the water's edge. "Can't Diarmid hurry? Can't he shout? Marcia, I shall die," piteously.

"No, you won't," holding firm the shaking shoulders. "He's coming as fast as he can. Look, the Superintendent's waving. That means it's all right. It must be all right. Anne-Louise, dare we call Kirsty?"

"I don't know. I'm frightened. I can't bear to see Sean hurt. If he's hurt — "

"You'll look after him, as you looked after those patients of your father's. You're not frightened of a few bruises or a patch of congealed blood. You've washed many nasty wounds without turning a hair. What you're afraid of, Anne-Louise, is that Sean may have given part of his love to his father. Is that it?"

"I suppose so," hollowly.

"You wouldn't have it otherwise, really," went on Marcia. In the pearly light of the dawn many things had been made clear: Diarmid saying: "We're going now," and her reply: "Bring him home, Diarmid. Tell him there's nothing to fear. Nobody's going to upheave his pasture again." He had taken her in his arms and kissed her. "Bless you," he said. "I'll find him and Sean," though she knew he had scant hope of the boy's survival. Yet now, when the boat had almost reached them, she was certain Sean was safe. A light was reflecting from the broken altar on Clunare, as the sun shone down on a storm-lashed world; some odd shaft had caught a stone, a piece of glass, a remnant of ancient pottery; it was flashing its message of hope to the tiny crowd. In the midst of unbelief, the holy island was giving a sign to the superstitious, that it carried its own secrets and guarded its own treasures. "He had to know his father before he could know himself. Without this, Anne-Louise, you would have had only half Sean. The other half would have been wandering uncommitted. Whatever he comes back, he comes back

318

in the knowledge that he did what he had to do and knowing that you wished him to go. Be thankful, my dear, that your trial has come early, not like Kirsty's and Padraig's, at the very end."

Kirsty was in the water, plunging towards the boat with a desperation that lent her strength, clinging to the gunwhale, looking down on what it contained. Diarmid had paused and put out his hands. The Superintendent, with rare understanding, got out of the boat and waded ashore and then stood guard while the ones who lay on the boards could look up and see a beloved face.

"I found him," said Sean. He sat awkwardly, nursing a broken rib, his face pitted and creased with pain, his hands torn where the rocks had battered him, his cheeks bruised and his lips cut where he had clenched them over his teeth. "I've brought him home to you."

The effect was almost too much. He twisted painfully and saw his mother bend lower, not over him, but over the man who lay, wrapped in the Superintendent's great coat and a grey woollen blanket, white as a bleached sheet, exhausted and frail, and he pushed down the illogical desire for her smile of approval, closed his eyes against the glory of the love that was transcending the lined, grey cheeks. Odd, he thought vaguely, wandering off down paths of excruciating pain, how women forgot the smarts, how once having chosen their mate they came back, asking for more, still loving. Would Anne-Louise . . . and smiled with the utter weariness of prostration and did not complain.

Kirsty took the thin cold body in her arms and held it against her bosom. Crooningly, she murmured words of love and promise and stroked the hollow temples, put her lips to the closed eyelids and breathed warmth into the frozen lips, found strength in her wet, sodden limbs to hold that which had been salved from the wreckage.

"Little love, come to me. Come to my arms and find your rest. Find warmth and a full heart where you found it always, where it always was, though it failed you, Padraig, and ran away from you and left you empty. 'Tis warm you are, in Kirsty's arms. Kirsty's here, holding you, giving you back your humanity, your belief in yourself. Kirsty O'Halloran, the while! You remember, my love, coming to her cottage and asking her, barely eighteen and with the hurt of your father on you, and the possession of great things. They can be yours still, alanna, in the respected buildings of Dublin, away from the narrow streets and the cobbles."

Nonsense, she was saying, to get the warmth back to his nostrils, the awareness to his eyes. Nonsense and the language of lovers, in a mixture of consoling and praying and entreating and longing, to parry the departed years that had stamped their mark on them.

"You'll find me older, Padraig, an old harridan that's learned a lot of sense since she went with you to Dublin and ran away to England and came to Dunphilly to torment you by learning the Latin. That would touch you, the frozen mould of a Riall, thinking to prick the sanctity of your scholarship. Kirsty O'Halloran knowing the Latin. The impudence of the woman! 'Twas knowing the Latin though, that gave us the clue and got you back in one piece instead of as a corpse. Is it listening you are, Padraig, while I torture myself the while, or is it sleeping you be, on that rough tumbled altar, or flat stone of your mother? What would you have with either? Cuimin's dead, these hundreds of years, and saint though he is, and nobody's going to tell Kirsty O'Halloran he is not, he has nothing to tell us the now. We've been behind the veil, the two of us; we know the blackness there is, and the awful loneliness and the bleakness, and the wonder of the return. You'll know it now, Padraig, how it was, when I came from Clunare and you would have nothing of me. You'll know it was the hand that was outstretched . . . the hand that is holding you now, perforce. There's nothing so comforting as a secret shared. We'll have no need of Clunare now, and Cuimin can rest in his holy place, and we'll have Marchmont. 'Tis big enough, the mansion, and I'd be content in a smaller house but you'd not want to leave the stones, save to go to Trinity, to be a scholar, betimes. Padraig Riall," she said, holding his face to hers, touching his cheek with hers, passing her words to his lips and into his resuscitating breath, "is it never you're going to reply, after this long time in the cold, the utter sinners we are and the biggest pair of fools . . ."

The gaunt head stirred beneath her touch.

"If it's Kirsty you want as she was when she went, you can have her. She's waiting behind the door in Dunphilly. If you'd gone in once, little love, you'd have seen her, with the bloom on her cheeks, the mother of the boy who's the spit image of you, even to his weird notions and his high-flying love. A time I've had of it with him, and never a father's hand to form him, till today when he swam the rough water and climbed the wild path and found you with Cuimin, the blessed saint, the friend of the strayed and the weak. We'll put a cross to St. Cuimin where I and then you found our strength. It'll be a thank-offering for the years that are to be, and we'll leave him his Book that he may read it to other travellers who are led to his care. Isn't that the way, Padraig, to learn from one's ills and take what is given one?"

The eyelids quivered. She kissed them, one by one, tenderly, with a love born of that shining clean-swept morning.

"Come to me, alanna. Say that you are

with me, who dragged you down and now would drag you up, who isn't worth your mother, the blessed one, but is the only person you loved in your blind innocence, your awakened joy."

The eyelids were open. The grey eyes were looking at the bent, lined face into which a measure of rejuvenescence had come, to offset the scare of the fashing night, and seeing a hope, a faint light at the end of a tunnel, a shape of a cross on a broken altar. He stirred, and she held him closer, and smiled the smile of his mother, and Saint Cuimin, and all the blessed ones in heaven, and then, he wasn't sure, he had been so far, it was a long way back, but it looked like Kirsty, Kirsty with another face and a calmer, deeper voice, Kirsty with arms that were holding him not pushing him away, Kirsty who had come near, so near . . . the Kirsty he had sought in his loneliest, blackest moments, the Kirsty who had lived so close, only eight miles away and would not speak, who had asked to come to him once and been denied . . . the Kirsty he had dreamt might come, nevertheless, if he would only call . . .

"Kirsty," he muttered, and the shaft of light on Clunare rose up to the sky and was lost in the radiance, one with the glitter of the heavens. "Kirsty. Is it Kirsty?" He sighed. He tried to smile, such a poor, feeble attempt at a smile, that she could not stay the tears that ran down her cheeks and paired themselves with his. "Ah!" he said; then a pain that had been in his forehead subsided. "I ran away," he confessed.

"I came after you," she told him. "We've changed the positions and we're quits. We go on from here together, Padraig and Kirsty; we'll not be so foolish again as to put our faith in bogus things. We'll keep to the firm ground and take a new hold of ourselves and know it's silly to wander. And now, betimes, you want a hot bed and warm food, and a month of good nursing before I'll allow you to so much as put a foot to the floor, Padraig Riall of Marchmont Royal, the sweet, foolish man that you are."

"Anne-Louise," said Sean, "I'm all right. Don't cry, my darling." He held her sobbing, hysterical body close to his broken rib. "I'm a bit knocked about. The tide was high and the skiff was strange and that blessed saint didn't seem to want me to get to his island, confound him, but I was going there. Nothing was going to stop me, not after they'd told me not to go. A good thing I did too. He was lying on a stone with nothing to shield him from the weather and he was soaked through and shivering and in a panic lest he was lost. Funny, wasn't it, when he'd gone there to return the Book and knew it was Cuimin's island. I suppose when you get in that state you don't know what you're doing. I was in a state, wasn't I, but because they stayed and waited and did nothing until it had cleared. He would have been dead by then. I took some brandy and kept giving him sips and in between we talked. All the fight had gone out of him. He thanked me for going." Suddenly, his voice cracked. "Thanked me, Anne-Louise, who's been thinking harsh things of him all my life, beating up a hatred of him and all he had done. He told me, when he wasn't wandering, while we crouched in Cuimin's altar — I pulled away some more stones so I could get him in — and it was as Diarmid said, at Winter's Grace, and I saw that it wasn't natural to go harbouring a wrong. He was sorry for his spitefulness and I told him a few things he didn't enjoy but I hadn't liked others, I said, and he saw the point — he's not so bad, after all, when you get him to see; like all the grown-ups, determined to think we are kids — and he told me about Marchmont and what he hoped I would do when I was married and I told him about you and he wants to see you, when he's better. He won't hurt you, Anne-Louise. He won't hurt anyone again. He's had his lesson. Do you know how? It's odd how some minds work. You'd think all this un-happiness over the years would be enough. No, it was up there, he said, when he got there, after he'd almost drowned in the bay, and the dip in the dell was out of the storm, and he realised he was alive, and Cuimin . . ."

"Don't tell me he came to him, as he did to your mother," Anne-Louise said in a mixture of scorn and helplessness, her voice hovering on the edge of disbelief.

"Up there," continued Sean, "you can believe anything. When my rib's better,

I'll take you and you'll see. There's a powerful spirit hovering over that island and I'm not disputing that if people say they've seen the saint they haven't. I'm not disputing the works of God, Anne-Louise, and neither are you, when you see them over there, my mother and my father who have been estranged . . ." Again, his voice cracked. "Anne-Louise," pleadingly; the cry for help was intense, for one last reassurance.

She gave it to him. "We won't ever be estranged, Sean," she promised, "and if you like when we have a son we'll call him Cuimin," shyly, for she was hardly yet sure of her love.

"Darling — " he stuttered while the wonder was in his eyes as he swayed from the pain of his cuts and bruises, and she supported him, her lips tender and sweet. "Darling Anne-Louise," he breathed happily.

The terrace was quiet, facing the south and the dig. The fallen branches of the oak lay in a chaos of tangle and wreckage across the corner of the garden; elsewhere there was evidence of the passing of the storm.

Through the gap between the Reek and the Pins, Clunare was shrouded in mist, guarding its secret. To Marcia, by the flaking balustrade, came Diarmid.

"I built it up and made a rough cross and placed it over the spot where I'd buried the Book. It won't fall open again for a hundred years."

It was what they had agreed should be done, he and she and Kirsty and Sean, and tomorrow he would tell the world that the precious Book was back with its owner, on the holy island where it had been used.

"Men and women can stand at his shrine and know the story of his Book but nobody else's hands are going to touch it, and the Rialls that shall be shall guard it, jealously, with their lives, because of the miracles it has wrought and the joy it has brought out of anguish. Over there, Marcia, with only the gulls and my mother's grave for my witnesses, it seemed that that was what should be, to ensure the peace that comes at the end of long striving. She found her peace. Kirsty and Padraig and Sean have found their peace. Before we leave, will you come with me to Clunare?"

"Yes, Diarmid," she said. "When you

were gone to fetch Padraig, I couldn't bear it lest anything had happened to you — "

He took her in his arms and held her close.

THE END

The Publisher will be delighted to send you, free of charge, upon request a complete and up-to-date list of all titles available.

Ulverscroft Large Print Books Ltd.
The Green, Bradgate Road
Anstey, Leicester
England